CHIAROSCURO

Luigi Pascal Rondanini

Copyright © 2025 Luigi Pascal Rondanini

All rights reserved

The characters and events portrayed in this book are fictitious. Any similarity to real persons, living or dead, is coincidental and not intended by the author.

No part of this book may be reproduced, or stored in a retrieval system, or transmitted in any form or by any means, electronic, mechanical, photocopying, recording, or otherwise, without express written permission of the publisher.

*To those who refuse to remain invisible, build bridges between worlds, and choose love over fear.
May their stories continue to emerge from shadow into light.*

CONTENTS

Title Page
Copyright
Dedication
Chapter 1   1
Chapter 2   27
Chapter 3   41
Chapter 4   54
Chapter 5   72
Chapter 6   96
Chapter 7   117
Chapter 8   125
Chapter 9   138
Chapter 10   146
Author's Note   168
Thank You for Reading!   170
Acknowledgement   171
About The Author   173

CHAPTER 1

Lorenzo Moretti had seen many patterns in numbers over the years—growth rates, recession indicators, the ebb and flow of credit approvals.

But this? This wasn't just an irregularity. It was deliberate.

Lorenzo paused in his calculations, catching his reflection in the darkened computer screen. He drummed his fingers against the desk, staring at the endless column of figures. Each approval was too clean, too swift—like a stamp pressed down without thought. He had spent years in control, trusting numbers over intuition, yet this unease gnawed at him in a way he couldn't ignore.

Lorenzo's fingers grazed his tie, a once-comforting ritual now as stifling as the too-small collar that chafed his neck. He tugged at the knot, desperate for air, but found no relief.

Someone was tampering with the approvals. Lorenzo flipped through the files again, his pulse quickening. Page after page, Giorgio's signature stood out, identical in its sharp slant. Too identical. He exhaled sharply, his gut churning—whoever had done this wanted Giorgio's name woven through every thread of this mess.

'*Direttore?* Still working?' Marina stood in the doorway, her silhouette sharp against the dim hallway light. For a split second she hesitated before stepping forward. The crispness of her blouse was at odds with the slight tremor in her voice

'These approval rates for the Trastevere district—they're thirty per cent higher than usual.'

'The economy is improving,' Marina offered, but something in her tone made him look up. She shifted slightly, her professional smile not quite reaching her eyes. 'Giorgio approved the new guidelines himself.'

'Did he?' Lorenzo returned to the documents, memorising the details. Giorgio had been making several unilateral decisions lately, each one just within his authority, yet collectively forming a pattern that gnawed at Lorenzo's instincts.

***

Once back, the key turned in the lock of his modestly furnished apartment. Inside, art prints transformed the walls into a personal gallery, each piece carefully chosen and positioned. Rosa, his Ecuadorian housekeeper, was tending to the potted plants on his neglected balcony, her experienced hands working with quiet efficiency.

She looked up at his arrival, her eyes crinkling with familiar warmth. '*Signor* Moretti, these plants need more attention than just my three weekly visits,' she said, brushing soil from her hands. 'They're like people—they need care, conversation.'

Lorenzo's gaze swept across his apartment, taking in the vast collection of art books lining the shelves. 'They're lucky to have your care at all, Rosa—like everything else in this apartment.'

'Everything except you,' she replied, stepping inside to gather her cleaning supplies. The broom made soft, sweeping sounds against the floor as she worked. 'Life isn't meant to be lived alone, *Signor* Moretti,' Rosa said, her voice tinged with concern.

'You think you're content, but you don't see the life you're missing.'

'My books are my companions,' Lorenzo said, loosening his tie. 'Numbers during the day; art in the evening—it's enough for me.' He settled at his kitchen table, where he took his evening meals, carefully placing his papers in the same spot he methodically did every morning.

Rosa paused in her work, leaning on her broom. 'Perhaps the company of real people? The warmth of friendship?' she hesitated, then pressed on. 'María is having a farewell party this weekend in Rocca Priora. She's moving back to Ecuador with her husband—' Rosa said, her tone softening.

'Rosa—'

'Just listen, *por favor*,' she said, moving closer, her voice taking on an urgent tone. 'It would mean so much if you came to Rocca Priora. These gatherings, they remind me of home, of my childhood.' Her voice softened. 'Ten years I've been here, working to bring the family to Italy. And now, finally—'

'Your family is coming?' Lorenzo's expression softened slightly.

'*Sí, esperamos que sí*.' Rosa's eyes brightened with hope. 'Finally. Which is why María's party is so special. She found a way to return home, to keep her family together.' Her hands stilled on the broom handle. 'My child, my husband—I've missed so much. But soon...'

'I understand your joy, Rosa, but—'

'No, you don't understand,' Rosa said, emotion causing her to mumble something inaudible shifting between Italian and Spanish.

Lorenzo studied the woman who had become more than just his housekeeper, noting the genuine concern in her eyes.

'Rosa, I appreciate your kind invitation, *pero* you know how I am. I prefer—'

She touched his arm gently. 'I know—you prefer Caravaggio's light and shadow to the light and shadow of real life.'

With practised efficiency, she gathered her cleaning supplies, preparing to leave.

'But if you ever change your mind, there will always be a place for you among friends.'

After Rosa left, Lorenzo sat at his kitchen table, the flavours of his solitary meal barely registering

***

Lorenzo pushed through the heavy doors of the Scuderie del Quirinale, the sudden chill of marble embracing him like an old friend. The hushed reverence of the space settled over him, the echoes of his footsteps swallowed by centuries of art and history.

The hushed reverence of the Caravaggio exhibition offered respite, the faint scent of old paint and the weight of centuries hanging in the air.

A painting pulled him in, its *chiaroscuro* strokes cutting through the darkness like a blade. A saint's face loomed from shadow, eyes lifted in agony, a silent cry frozen in oil and time. Lorenzo leaned closer, his breath shallow—Caravaggio had captured something raw, something dangerously familiar.

He leaned closer to the Caravaggio, studying the interplay of light and shadow that made the saint's face seem to emerge from darkness.

His fingers twitched, aching to trace the masterful brushstrokes.

***

'*Signore?*'

A small voice broke through his concentration. '*Scusi, signore?*'

He turned, ready to dismiss the interruption, but found only empty air at eye level. Lowering his eyes, he saw a boy, no more than nine, clutching a museum guide with white-knuckled fingers, below him.

'I can't—' The boy's voice cracked. '*Non riesco a trovare la mia mamma.*'

Something in the child's expression—terror barely held at bay by determination—made Lorenzo kneel to his level, despite his precisely pressed trousers.

Lorenzo crouched to the boy's level, his voice lowering instinctively. 'You can't find your mother?' He hadn't meant for it to sound so soft, so careful—yet the boy's frightened eyes pulled something unfamiliar from him.

Around them, the galleries hummed with quiet conversations and shuffling footsteps.

'What's your name?' Lorenzo asked gently.

'Miguel Blanco,' the scared boy replied.

'Nice to meet you, Mr Blanco. I'm Lorenzo Moretti, but you can call me Lorenzo,' the banker replied with a genuine smile on his face.

Lorenzo experienced an unexpected surge of protectiveness.

He placed a steady hand on the boy's shoulder.

'Of course I'll help you find her.'

'Which gallery did you last see your mother in?' Lorenzo asked, keeping his voice calm while scanning the growing crowd of concerned museum staff.

'The one with the angels.' Miguel's hand found Lorenzo's sleeve, fingers twisting in the expensive fabric. 'She was talking to a man—'

He stopped abruptly, something flickering across his face that Lorenzo recognised from years of evaluating loan applicants. Fear of saying too much.

'What kind of man?'

Lorenzo kept his tone casual, but his banker's instincts sharpened.

'Like you. In a suit.' Miguel's grip tightened. 'But not like you. You look at the paintings like mi Abuelo in Ecuador.' The boy's voice steadied slightly. 'The other man… he wasn't looking at the art at all.'

'Let me tell you something about the *Chiaroscuro* technique—' Lorenzo was interrupted in his words.

A woman's voice cut through the gallery—'Miguel!'—and the boy's face transformed with relief.

She emerged from the Byzantine gallery like a Caravaggio figure stepping from shadow into light. Her professional attire—conservative suit, modest heels—but something in her bearing suggested deeper complexity. Dark eyes swept the scene, assessing Lorenzo even as she moved toward her son.

'¡Miguel! ¡*Gracias a Dios!*' Her voice carried controlled panic, the kind Lorenzo had heard from clients in the moments before revealing financial disasters.

Miguel released Lorenzo's sleeve but didn't run to his mother immediately. Instead, he looked up at Lorenzo.

'This is the man who helped me, Mama. He knows about art, like *Abuelo*.'

She reached them in three quick steps, one hand going to Miguel's shoulder while the other extended toward Lorenzo.

'Camila Velasco,' she said, her accent refined, diplomatic. 'I cannot thank you enough, *Signor*...?'

'Moretti. Lorenzo Moretti.'

As Lorenzo introduced himself, Camila's fingers tightened almost imperceptibly on Miguel's shoulder, her nails pressing crescents into the fabric of his shirt.

'Your son has excellent taste in art for his age.'

'Yes,' she said, something guarded entering her expression. 'His grandfather's influence. He's an art lover.'

The warm embraces resembled a comforting hug, as Lorenzo was swept away in a whirlwind of gratitude, the sounds of happy chatter filling his ears. As Miguel's mother thanked him profusely, he perceived the careful walls of his solitude beginning to crack.

'The Caravaggio exhibition is exceptional,' Camila said, her eyes moving between Lorenzo and the exits. 'Though I prefer his Roman period to the Maltese works.'

'The use of light is more dramatic in the Roman pieces,' Lorenzo agreed, noting how she positioned herself between Miguel and the passing crowds. 'The shadows tell as much of the story as the illuminated portions.'

'Yes,' she said, something flickering in her expression. 'Shadows can reveal more than light, can't they, *Signor* Moretti?'

Before he had a chance to answer, a man in a dark suit arrived at the gallery entrance, speaking rapidly into a phone. Camila's posture shifted subtly—a change so slight Lorenzo might have missed it if he hadn't spent decades reading body language across negotiating tables.

'We should go,' she said, her tone professionally pleasant but firm. 'Miguel has homework waiting, don't you, *mijo*?'

Miguel looked up from the exhibition catalogue he'd been showing Lorenzo. 'But Mama, *Signor* Moretti was going to explain about the *Chiaroscuro* technique—'

'Another time, perhaps.' She smiled at Lorenzo, but her eyes remained watchful. 'Thank you again for your help.'

As they turned to leave, Lorenzo caught a glimpse of the man in the suit speaking to a security guard, gesturing in their direction. The guard shook his head, pointing toward a different gallery.

***

Lorenzo's phone buzzed as he entered his apartment that evening.

A text from an unknown number: *Unusual activity in Trastevere accounts. Check file B394. -M*

Who's this? Was his reply.

It's Marina, direttore.

Marina had never contacted him after hours before.

He poured a glass of wine and strolled toward his study.

Once connected to the bank's SharePoint, he pulled the relevant file, spreading the documents across his desktop. The approval signatures looked correct, but something about the routing numbers...

***

His landline rang, startling him. Only Rosa had that number.

'*Signor* Moretti,' her voice was hushed. 'I'm sorry to call so late, but there's something you should know about the consulate.'

'Which consulate? What is it?'

'My cousin's friend—the one who works in the Ecuadorian visa section—she said someone's been asking questions about you. About your banking department specifically.'

'Why the Ecuadorian consulate? When did this happen?'

'Last week. And *Signor* Moretti...' Rosa paused. 'The man asking? He works for Silvio Bianchi.'

The name hung in the air like smoke. Bianchi's reputation in Rome's financial circles was complicated—a successful businessman on paper, but whispers suggested darker enterprises.

Lorenzo looked at Marina's text again, then at the loan documents. The routing numbers matched accounts he'd flagged last month—accounts tied to businesses in Trastevere that Giorgio had personally approved.

'Grazie, Rosa,' he said. 'I may need your help with something.'

He was thinking of Camila Velasco.

'Of course.' Her voice carried a hint of relief, as though she'd been waiting for this request. 'My network is your network, *Signor* Moretti. Just ... be careful. Some questions are dangerous to ask in Rome.'

***

The morning market at Campo de' Fiori was coming to life, vendors arranging their produce with practised care. The scents of fresh bread and coffee mingled with animated conversations.

He passed through Piazza Farnese, the palazzo's Renaissance façade overlooking the square as it had for centuries.

At the Sisto Bridge, Lorenzo paused, his gaze drawn to Castel Sant'Angelo. Stones layered like memories. A monument to forgotten emperors and popes, Hadrian's tomb, now a papal fortress, stood heavy with the weight of its own past, its stones cold and ancient. 'Purpose changes, but essence remains, like human hearts constantly remaking themselves,' he told himself.

***

Lorenzo arrived at the bank earlier than usual, that morning, before even the cleaning staff. He needed time with the files before Marina or Giorgio appeared.

Lorenzo scrolled through the approval logs, cross-referencing the account numbers. The pattern was too precise—too controlled. The same sequence of approvals, the same set of routing numbers, all funnelling through businesses that barely had a presence.

He frowned, clicking on a flagged transaction. The documents were pristine, each signature flawlessly placed.

Too flawless.

***

A cold certainty settled over him. Someone had preemptively structured these loans to evade suspicion—not just careless fraud, but deliberate engineering.

His phone vibrated. Marina.

Meet me in the archives. You need to see this in person. 6PM.

The weight of her message was clear. If she was reaching out like this, something was deeply wrong.

And if he was right, Giorgio wasn't just approving these loans.

As Lorenzo stepped into the bank's archives, the musty scent of decades-old paper and the faint tang of ink assailed his nostrils. The air hung heavy with the weight of countless forgotten transactions, each one a silent witness to the institution's history. He followed Marina past rows of filing cabinets, their footsteps echoing in the basement silence. She stopped at a section marked 2024—Approved Commercial Loans.

'Watch,' she said, pulling out a file. 'Notice anything about these signatures?'

Lorenzo examined the document. Giorgio's signature looked perfect—identical to the one above it, and the one above that. Exactly identical.

'They're forgeries?'

'Extremely good ones. But look at the dates.' Marina pulled out more files. 'These were all approved while Giorgio was supposedly in Milan for that conference.'

A door slammed somewhere above them. Marina jumped, nearly dropping the files.

'Someone's been accessing these records after hours,' she continued, her voice shaking. 'With credentials that shouldn't exist. I tracked the logins to—'

Footsteps on the stairs cut her off. She shoved the files back into place.

'The wrong question at the wrong time can cost you more than your job,' she whispered.

The footsteps grew closer. Lorenzo moved to block the files from view as Giorgio appeared at the end of the row.

'Ah, Moretti,' he said, his smile not reaching his eyes. 'Sharing another history lesson with Marina?'

He giggled referring to the amount of paper kept in that storage space, part of a not so distant past.

'Showing her the old filing system,' Lorenzo replied smoothly. 'Historical context for our digital transition.'

'How thorough of you.' Giorgio's gaze swept over them. 'Tomorrow, the board meeting's starting early. Have fun, you two?'

***

Marina's hand hovered over Lorenzo's desk, the steam from the espresso curling around her fingers like a question mark. Her lips parted, words forming and dissolving in the space between them, before she finally set the cup down with a soft clink.

'You've been working late these days, *direttore*,' she said, forcing a smile. 'Burning yourself out over these files?'

Lorenzo studied her. The warmth in her voice was still there, but something was off. A stiffness in her posture. A flicker of hesitation when their eyes met.

'Comes with the territory,' he said lightly. 'Besides, I have a feeling this is bigger than we think.'

She stilled for a fraction of a second, barely noticeable—unless you were watching for it.

'Bigger how?' she asked, too casually.

He tapped a file. 'These approvals—someone's been manufacturing perfect transactions. As if they knew exactly what compliance would flag.'

A small laugh. Too small. 'Maybe we're just seeing ghosts.'

Lorenzo leaned back. 'Maybe. Yesterday you seemed to agree.'

Marina didn't reply.

'Anyway, it's time to attend the board meeting. You'll be there? Right?'

***

The boardroom's floor-to-ceiling windows offered a perfect view of Rome's skyline, but Lorenzo's attention was fixed on the documents before him.

Giorgio was presenting the quarterly results, his voice confident as he detailed their record-breaking loan approval rates.

'Our new streamlined process has increased efficiency by forty per cent,' Giorgio announced. 'The Trastevere district alone—'

'About that,' Lorenzo interrupted, ignoring Marina's warning glance from the corner where she took notes. 'I've been reviewing those applications.'

'Something's missing in these files—not a mistake, but a gap. The data is too clean, too controlled.'

Silence fell over the room. Giorgio's smile tightened almost imperceptibly.

'Unusual how?'

'The response times, the documentation quality—everything's too perfect. As if someone had foreseen exactly what we needed before we asked.'

'Are you suggesting impropriety?' Giorgio's tone was light, but his eyes hardened. 'Perhaps you're just unused to efficient processes, Lorenzo. Not everything needs to move at the pace of your art appreciation.'

Nervous laughter rippled around the table. Lorenzo noticed the board members' gazes shift between them like spectators at a tennis match.

'I'm suggesting,' Lorenzo said carefully, 'that we might want to audit the new system. For security purposes.'

'Motion denied,' Giorgio said smoothly. 'We've already exceeded our compliance budget for the quarter. Now, moving on to our expansion plans...'

Lorenzo caught Marina's eye across the room. She gave a tiny nod toward her tablet, where a message flashed briefly: My office. 6 PM.

He never saw her. By 6 PM, Marina had left.

***

Back at home, he found Rosa standing in the doorway, her usual efficiency replaced by an unusual thoughtfulness.

'You seem lost in thought,' Lorenzo observed, heading toward his study.

Rosa's hands stilled on her cleaning cloth. 'I was thinking of home,' she said softly. 'Did you know I grew up with twelve siblings in Quito?'

Lorenzo set down his jacket on a chair by the door, before sitting behind his mahogany desk.

'Thirteen children? That must have been...'

'Chaotic?' Rosa's laugh carried warmth despite its weariness.

'Yes, but wonderful too. Our house was tiny, and we had so little money. But *Mamá* somehow made it work. She managed to stretch a pot of soup to feed fifteen people. We shared everything —beds, clothes, toys. Nobody minded.'

Rosa's eyes drifted to the window, her gaze unfocusing as if she were watching scenes from a distant.

'At night, *Papá* would gather us around our only lantern to read stories. He did different voices for each character. Even now, I can hear him.'

Lorenzo leaned back, studying her expression. 'Yet you left all that behind.'

'Not by choice, at first.' Rosa's hands tightened on the shelf she was dusting. 'When I was sixteen, floods destroyed everything. We lived on rice and beans for months. But even then, my parents insisted we stay in school. "*La educación es lo único que no pueden quitarte,*" *Papá* would say—education is the one thing they can't take from you.'

'They sound like remarkable people.'

'They are.' Rosa's voice softened. 'At twenty-three, I faced the biggest decision of my life. I had just married Pacho, my childhood sweetheart, and we had our beautiful Itzamná.'

'Your son,' Lorenzo murmured, watching how her expression changed at the mention of her child.

Rosa nodded, blinking rapidly. 'I left them behind to come here, hoping to send money home. The journey...' She paused, collecting herself. 'The journey was difficult, but I had no choice.'

***

'Is that when you started working as a cleaner?'

'Any work I could find—living in crowded rooms with other immigrant women, sending every spare euro home.' Her hands trembled slightly. 'After two years, I finally saved enough to visit. Itzamná … he barely knew me.'

Lorenzo shifted in his chair, discomfort evident in his posture.

'That must have been devastating.'

'It was. But by then…' Rosa turned to face him fully. 'I found work here. And you…' She gestured around his study. 'You changed everything when you helped me get my papers.'

'Anyone would have done the same,' Lorenzo murmured, embarrassed by her gratitude.

'No, they wouldn't.' Rosa's voice carried quiet conviction. 'Most people looked right through me. But you saw me as a person—not just another illegal immigrant.'

'You reminded me of my mother,' Lorenzo admitted softly. 'She always said one act of kindness could change a life.'

Rosa smiled, returning to her dusting. 'She was wise, your mother. I also care for *Signora* Martelli—the elderly lady in apartment 4B. She reminds me of the grandmother I never had. Sometimes, when she talks about her youth in Rome, I can almost imagine my own children growing up here someday.'

'So, you think Pacho and Itzamná will join you shortly?'

'I hope so—I pray for it every day.' Rosa touched the small cross at her neck, a gesture Lorenzo had noticed she made when speaking of her family. 'Until then, I keep working, sending money home, and building a life here. My heart is split between two worlds, but somehow, that makes it grow bigger, not smaller.'

Lorenzo nodded, understanding something about sacrifice he

hadn't before.

'Your family would be proud, Rosa—of the way you've built a bridge between those worlds.'

'Gracias.' Rosa's smile carried the warmth of her distant home. 'Sometimes bridges appear in the most unexpected places.'

***

As evening approached, the warm glow from a small cocktail bar near the Vatican walls drew Lorenzo in—its inviting atmosphere a stark contrast to the usual tourist traps he avoided.

Something about his encounter at the museum had shifted his usual patterns, making him more receptive to unexpected turns.

The bar's warmth and the bartender's practised movements drew him in, a contrast to his day's rigid formalities.

Seated at the bar, he studied the array of bottles lining the wall, each one representing a possibility he had never explored.

'Buonasera, signore. What can I prepare for you tonight?' the bartender asked warmly.

Lorenzo glanced at the impressive display before him and offered a small smile. 'I must confess, I know very little about cocktails. Perhaps you could surprise me with something of your choice?'

'This is my own creation,' she explained, setting down a beautifully garnished glass. 'The Soleil Kiss—a blend of rum, fresh citrus, and aromatic bitters. I think you'll find it intriguing.'

The bartender's expertise impressed him, each movement precise and purposeful. Like Marina's had been, he thought suddenly, remembering how efficiently she'd handled those loan documents. He pushed the thought away, but it tainted his first sip.

The cocktail's colours mirrored a Roman sunset.

The bar's energy swirled around him: laughter, conversation, and the gentle clink of glasses.

***

As hunger stirred, he pulled out his old Nokia phone—a remnant of his resistance to change. Perhaps it was time to step into the present; tomorrow he would look into upgrading to something more current.

His feet guided him through Trastevere's winding streets. The neighbourhood hummed with evening life, and the warm glow of a small corner restaurant caught his attention. Golden light spilled from its windows, carrying with it the aroma of garlic and herbs.

'Table for one this evening, sir?'

The host led him to a candlelit table outside at his nod.

The warmth of the *trattoria* should have been comforting, but Lorenzo had chosen a corner table, his back to the wall. Old habits from banking, he told himself, though these instincts seemed sharper now, more urgent.

The young host approached with genuine enthusiasm. 'Since it's your first visit, may I make some recommendations?'

'Please,' Lorenzo said, surprising himself with his openness to guidance.

The first bite of *supplì* revealed perfectly crisp risotto giving way to melting cheese. His *cacio e pepe* arrived with pasta cooked to precise al dente perfection, the silky pecorino sauce carrying just the right bite of black pepper.

***

The city seemed vibrant in ways he hadn't noticed before. Yet with each step, unbidden thoughts of Antonella drifted into his mind, her laughter echoing from another life.

In his early twenties, he had fallen hard for a fiery artist whose passion matched her vibrant paintings, the scent of oil paints ever present in her studio. Their time together had been a whirlwind of hushed gallery visits and sunlit afternoons in Neapolitan piazzas, filled with the scent of espresso and the sound of lively debate. But when Lorenzo chose a steady banking career over their shared dream of opening an art studio, Antonella left, taking with her the light that had illuminated his life.

Her departure had marked a reckoning—Lorenzo had chosen stability over love, fearing uncertainty more than he realised.

After her, he had retreated into the safe harbours of work and art,

Late that evening, as Lorenzo sat by his window with a glass of wine, his thoughts drifted to the growing unease that had settled in his chest. The once-comforting routines of his life—the carefully arranged art, the quiet evenings spent with a good book – now felt like a flimsy shield against the gathering storm. He felt inescapably drawn to this moment of reckoning by every decision and step he'd taken. Couples' and families' laughter reached Lorenzo, making him wonder if he'd sacrificed messy warmth for career security.

As he watched Camila's silhouette against the darkening sky, fear twisted in his gut. For a long time, he'd built emotional barriers, content with his meticulously planned existence. The possibility of losing her, and with it, this unexpected chance at something authentic, made Lorenzo realize how deeply he depended on her to make him feel accepted and understood. The prospect of resuming his empty, lonely routines and cold nights in his old life filled him with an unshakeable sense of dread.

Lorenzo's thoughts were underscored by accordion music floating up from the street. The copper glow of lamplight on cobblestones and the lingering scent of dinner caught his attention.

Miguel's innocent enthusiasm at the museum had cracked something open in him. Tonight's adventures—the cocktail bar, the restaurant, the easy conversations with strangers—had widened that crack further.

***

The glow of the computer screen cast harsh shadows across Lorenzo's face as he hunched over his desk, the late hour marked by the relentless ticking of the clock. His fingers hovered over his phone keyboard, to pull up Marina's messages once more.

Her sudden interest in helping him—it appeared staged. Then her apparent change of heart…it was puzzling.

The transaction logs from Trastevere stared back at him, their numbers forming patterns that made his stomach twist.

Sleep would not come easily tonight. Not with these questions burning in his mind. Not with the growing suspicion that his carefully ordered world was about to shatter. Tomorrow he would dig deeper, ask harder questions. But tonight, watching Rome's lights flicker through the gathering storm clouds, Lorenzo understood that thirty years of banking experience suggested one thing: this wouldn't end soon.

***

The familiar rhythm of Rosa's cleaning, usually a source of

comfort, had a different effect tonight. Each sweep of her broom made him start slightly. She paused in her work, studying him with the shrewd insight that came from years of observation.

'*Signor* Moretti,' she ventured, leaning on her broom. 'Something is different about you today.'

Lorenzo forced his attention back to the present. 'Just work matters, Rosa. Nothing to concern yourself with.'

'Rosa,' Lorenzo said, setting down his espresso. 'About your message yesterday—sorry I didn't reply—who was asking about me at the consulate?'

'My cousin Carmen cleans for a family in Parioli,' she began, her voice low. 'The husband works at the consulate. Last night she overheard a phone call about missing documents—diplomatic pouches that never reached their destination.'

'How does this connect to the bank?'

Rosa's fingers drummed a nervous pattern on the table.

'Carmen says a man mentioned your bank.' She hesitated. 'There's more. The cleaning staff at the consulate has changed recently. New people, with perfect papers but no connections to our community. Teresa, who's worked there for twelve years, says they speak Spanish with the wrong accent.'

Lorenzo leaned forward. 'Wrong how?'

'Like they learned it in school, not in the streets of Quito or Lima.' Rosa's eyes met his. 'We notice these things, *Signor* Moretti. When you spend your life being invisible, you learn to see what others miss.'

'I don't know anyone at the Consulate. Well … I know the boy's mother, but she didn't know me until a few days ago.' He stopped wondering. 'And how does your friend know about Bianchi?'

A small smile played at Rosa's lips.

'*Signor* Moretti, you bankers think you have networks? In ten years of cleaning homes in Rome, I've built something even your fancy security systems can't match. We're everywhere—the cleaning ladies, the gardeners, the delivery boys. We see everything, hear everything. And we talk.'

Lorenzo stared at her, reassessing everything he thought he knew about his housekeeper.

'And this network… it's all Ecuadorian?'

'Ecuadorian, Peruvian, Colombian—we take care of each other. We have to.' She straightened, pride evident in her bearing.

'The wealthy and powerful think we're invisible. That's their mistake. Nothing happens in Rome that our community doesn't know about. Not in homes, not in offices, not even in banks.'

'But why tell me?'

Rosa's expression softened.

'Because you saw me, *Signor* Moretti. When I needed help with my papers, you didn't just sign them—you asked about my family, remembered their names. People like that are rare in our world.' She paused, then added carefully, 'And now, perhaps, you need our help too.'

The implications of her words settled over him like a heavy cloak. His careful world of numbers and art suddenly seemed naïve compared to this invisible network of observers and whispers.

'So at this party…' he began.

'You'll meet others who might have useful information.' Rosa resumed her sweeping, her tone casual again. 'But be careful who you trust. Not everyone is happy about a banker asking questions.'

The warning in her voice was clear, yet somehow comforting. In a world where he was losing his bearings, Rosa's mysterious network seemed an unexpected lifeline.

The scent of lemon and pine filled the air as she gathered her cleaning supplies; Lorenzo, however, found his gaze drifting to the window.

The street below teemed with life—couples strolling arm in arm, friends gathering at cafés, families heading home together. When had he started viewing such ordinary scenes with envy?

His phone buzzed. Unknown number. His hand hovered over it before rejecting the call, heart racing slightly. Since when did unknown numbers make him nervous?

Seeking solace from his troubled thoughts, Lorenzo found himself drawn to the grand entrance of the Scuderie del Quirinale, its imposing façade a stark contrast to the turmoil within him; the quiet murmur of other visitors a gentle background hum as he approached the Caravaggio exhibition. One painting in particular captivated him, its dramatic interplay of light and shadow imbuing the saint's face with an almost tangible sense of emotion.

The exhibition's quiet was broken by a young couple's whispered argument. Lorenzo watched their reflection in the protective glass, remembering Antonella her passion, her disappointment, her final walk away from his careful plans. He'd chosen security then. Now, standing amid masterpieces of light and shadow, he wondered what else that choice had cost him.

※※※

On his way home, the warm buzz of *Chiaroscuro* failed to dispel his unease. Rome's evening streets seemed different somehow —both more alive and more threatening. Each shadow might conceal an observer, each passing stranger might be recording details.

He caught his reflection In a darkened shop window—when had he started looking so watchful? The careful banker was still there, but something else looked back at him now. Someone who had glimpsed behind the curtain and couldn't quite forget what he'd seen.

The shortcut home led Lorenzo past Gino's, where the familiar scent of rosemary and garlic drifted through the air. The restaurant's owner, a fellow Neapolitan, caught sight of him through the window and waved.

'Ehi, *Signò*! Where've you been hiding?' Gino called, stepping outside. 'I thought you'd abandoned us.'

Lorenzo hesitated, then smiled. 'Just exploring new paths.'

'*Ma dai!* Come in! Fresh *mozzarella di bufala* arrived this morning.'

The warmth of Gino's welcome was a reminder of the Naples Lorenzo carried within him. He took a seat at his usual table, the old routine settling around him like a well-worn coat. Gino placed a plate of *bruschetta* in front of him, eyes twinkling.

'So, *Signor Banchiere*, have you finally embraced modernity?'

He nodded at the sleek phone on the table.

'Next thing I know, you'll be posting my pasta on Instagram.'

Lorenzo chuckled, shaking his head.

'Not likely.'

'I can tell something's different about you.'

Gino leaned in slightly.

'Maybe it's time you were just Lorenzo, eh?'

Lorenzo sat back, considering the words. Perhaps Gino was right.

Savouring familiar childhood flavours evoked a poignant nostalgia in Lorenzo for his simple Neapolitan life. A world separated his family's warm, cluttered apartment from the sterile elegance of his Roman home, its immaculate surfaces and curated art. Yet, in moments like these, surrounded by the comforting scents and sounds of home, Lorenzo could almost imagine a different path—one where he'd stayed true to his roots, rather than chasing the cold, hard world of finance.

***

The city streets pulsed with an unfamiliar energy, the very air electric with whispers of transformation. Lorenzo's skin prickled with anticipation, each step carrying him closer to an uncertain future he could no longer ignore. The question was: would he allow the transformation, or would he remain in the security that had become a prison?

His apartment seemed emptier than usual on his return. The art prints that usually brought comfort now seemed to watch him with knowing eyes.

Later, the sounds of an accordion floated up from the street, Lorenzo sat with a glass of wine, watching night settle over Rome.

The certainty he once held was slipping away. Yet somehow, despite the danger he sensed lurking at its edges, a part of him welcomed the upheaval. Perhaps it was time to stop hiding behind careful routines and measured responses.

The music faded, leaving him with only his thoughts and the

soft tick of his watch. Tomorrow would bring new challenges, new possibilities. After many years, a nervous flutter of anticipation, a thrill of the unknown, made him look forward to the uncertainty.

CHAPTER 2

'*Signor* Lorenzo,' Rosa said the next morning, pausing in her cleaning. 'Have you considered what I said about the party?'

He turned from his window, where he'd been watching someone in a dark suit who'd passed by twice.

'Actually, yes. Will there be many people there?'

Rosa's face brightened with surprise and hope. 'Many from our community. María has been here twenty years—she knows everyone.' She hesitated, then added with careful casualness, 'Including some from the consulate.'

The way she spoke caused him to raise his gaze abruptly. 'The consulate?'

'Sí. Like Camila—Miguel's mother? The one you helped at the museum?' Rosa watched his reaction with shrewd eyes. 'She might be there.'

Lorenzo's pulse quickened at the mention of Camila. He recalled her grace under pressure, the complexity in her eyes that matched her son's.

'You know her well?'

'Our community takes care of its own,' Rosa said, her voice carrying layers of meaning. 'Especially those who need…help.'

It wasn't an answer to his direct question, but he didn't insist.

***

That evening, as Lorenzo reviewed his party preparations, his phone buzzed with a message from an unknown number. His thumb hovered over it before he checked—just his new phone company with a welcome text. When had he become so jumpy?

The next few days passed In a blur of anticipation and anxiety. Lorenzo realised he had been paying extra attention to details he'd normally ignore—the way people watched him at work, the patterns of cars parked outside his building, the tone of casual conversations.

***

Saturday arrived with brilliant sunshine, as though nature itself approved of his plans. Yet, as he prepared for the party in Rocca Priora, anxiety crept in. Rosa still hadn't confirmed whether Camila would attend, and her warnings about how people might perceive him as a banker weighed on his mind.

Lorenzo studied his reflection, tugging at his collar and smoothing invisible wrinkles. When had he become so meticulous, so uncertain? A jolt of anxiety shot through him; his heart hammered in his chest—a frantic rhythm that mirrored the dampness spreading across his freshly ironed shirt. He wondered if his unease stemmed from the thrill of seeing Camila or the chilling uncertainty of entering an unfamiliar place. With a frustrated sigh, he changed his shirt once again.

***

The hours passed with no word from Rosa about the party details. When he finally managed to navigate to his email app spam folder, he found her message waiting—directions to a venue along the scenic Tuscolana road from Grottaferrata to

Rocca Priora. The options were clear: thirty-three minutes by car or fifty-five by public transport. Lorenzo opted for a taxi, sparing himself the additional stress of navigating buses and metros.

As he scrolled through photos of the venue, a memory stirred—he had been in this area before, though the details of that abandoned excursion remained hazy. The photos depicted a charming place—a bridge connecting his past and present, mirroring his own journey.

***

In the taxi, he started wondering. What would he say to Camila? How would she respond to seeing him again? And why did these social anxieties appear connected to his professional concerns?

The journey from Piazza Farnese to San Giovanni unfolded smoothly, the car gliding through Rome's narrow streets before merging into wider thoroughfares. The cobblestones gave way to asphalt as they left the historic centre. Lorenzo watched the city recede, each kilometre taking him further from his familiar world of careful control.

As they veered onto the Tuscolana Road, the landscape shifted subtly. The dense, timeworn façades of the city gave way to rows of modest shops, cafés, bakeries, the contrasting massive IKEA and Carrefour.

Urban bustle gave way to the rolling charm of the Castelli Romani countryside. Lorenzo cracked the window, letting in the earthy scent of sun-warmed soil and the faint hint of pine from the nearby woods. Each mile seemed to carry him further from his concerns about the bank, yet somehow also closer to new uncertainties.

The car climbed gently towards Rocca Priora, the air growing cooler with each turn. The flickering lights of Grottaferrata appeared briefly on the horizon, shimmering like stars before being swallowed again by the shadows of the hills. From somewhere unseen, the faint toll of a church bell punctuated the hum of the car engine.

***

When the taxi finally pulled up to the venue, the warm evening air was alive with the pulse of Latin American music drifting from within.

Lorenzo stepped out, adjusting his jacket against the breeze. But before he could reach the entrance, movement in his peripheral vision caught his attention—children playing in a nearby playground, their laughter rising above the music.

The sight of the boy sent a fresh wave of perspiration down his skin. He stood frozen for a moment, torn between his anticipation of seeing Camila and this unexpected reunion with her son. The music drew him in.

He finally entered, and a kaleidoscope of colour and motion exploded before him. The sounds of music and excited voices filled his ears. The room pulsed with warmth and music. Conversations flowed freely. Laughter rose above the rhythmic beat.

The atmosphere buzzed with easy laughter and familiarity, both welcoming and overwhelming.

He ventured into the crowd, letting the blend of Spanish and Italian conversations wash over him like waves. He was still orienting himself when Rosa's enthusiastic embrace surprised him.

'You came!' she beamed, pulling him eagerly through the crowd. 'Camila's here—she's helping with drinks right now. And María can't wait to meet you! I've told her so much about you over the years.'

He barely had time to process this information before Rosa brought him to María, the party's host. She greeted him warmly, dismissing his thanks for the invitation. 'Rosa has spoken of you so much that I have the impression that I already know you!'

As Rosa introduced him to one guest after another, he struggled to keep track of names and faces, offering smiles and broken Spanish greetings. His attention kept drifting to the bar, where Camila gracefully served drinks. When she finally had a moment to serve him a small shot, her apologetic smile carried a promise: 'I'll find you later when I've finished here.'

The party swirled around him—a vibrant tapestry of cultures and connections. The initial prickle of unease he had as an outsider softened as he sat with Rosa and six others, the warmth of their conversation melting his apprehension. When the rapid Spanish became overwhelming, they kindly switched to Italian.

'A banker!' one guest exclaimed when Lorenzo mentioned his profession. He was suddenly fielding questions about money transfers and loans, a comfortable familiarity washing over him as he discussed his work, the weight of his office chair absent from his shoulders.

Not all comments about banks and bankers were so flattering, though. A few complained about the rigidity of the system when it came to loans, for example. Lorenzo had no desire to contradict them by explaining rules and regulations, and he simply nodded, showing his understanding. As toasts and shared plates flowed, Lorenzo grew comfortable—until Rosa tugged at his arm with a mischievous smile.

'Come on!' she urged, eyes sparkling. 'Show us your moves!'

He hadn't even opened his mouth to object when a strong hand pulled him onto the brightly lit, pulsating dance floor. Years of self-imposed restraint fell away as the music flowed through him. His body remembered rhythms he thought long forgotten, and for a few precious moments, each step on the dance floor marked another wall coming down—the rigid banker transforming into someone who could embrace life's spontaneity.

Miguel's influence had started this change.

Then, Camila appeared before him, moving with natural grace. Their gaze locked, and the crowd faded.

'You're quite the dancer,' she said, with genuine admiration in her voice. 'Professional training?'

He laughed, shaking his head. 'Pure instinct, I promise you.'

Her smile made his heart skip. When she suggested finding somewhere quieter to talk, he followed without hesitation.

***

The evening air greeted them, carrying the faint scent of the sea drifting from beyond the hills.

His eyes instinctively scanned for Miguel, which made Camila smile.

'The children are safe,' she assured him. 'There's a clown entertaining them in the next room.'

She offered him a cigarette, and, although he hadn't smoked in decades, Lorenzo accepted. His first drag resulted in an embarrassing cough, eliciting a melodious laugh from Camila.

She smoked quietly beside him, her gaze fixed on the distant sea sparkling between the hills.

In the night's quiet embrace, Lorenzo's earlier anxieties faded, replaced by a deepening connection with Camila.

'The consul's wife gave me the tickets at the last minute,' she explained. 'If not for that, we might never have met.'

'The universe works in mysterious ways,' Lorenzo agreed, watching the smoke from her cigarette curl into the night air.

'It certainly does.' Her voice grew thoughtful. 'You know, when I first came to Italy, I never imagined forming such connections here.'

'What brought you to Rome?' he asked softly.

She took a long drag of her cigarette before answering.

'That's quite a story. I come from a prominent Ecuadorian family,' she said. 'My father, an army general, expected nothing less than excellence from his six children.'

'That must have been challenging,' he said.

'The challenge came later,' she said, her voice taking on a different tone. 'I fell in love with an army officer, Jorge, and ran away against my family's wishes,' she admitted. 'Our most fervent wishes often lead to lessons we couldn't foresee'

He noticed a subtle change In her posture. 'What happened?'

'He …' she hesitated. 'He turned out to be different from what I expected. Miguel's pregnancy gave me the strength to leave. My parents …' Her voice softened with gratitude. 'They welcomed me back without question.'

'That must have taken immense strength,' he interjected, managing to hide his excitement, as Rosa had mentioned they were still in a complicated relationship.

'When you're protecting your child, you find strength you never knew you had.' Camila's smile returned. 'Then came the opportunity—the consul needed a personal assistant who spoke French and English. It seemed like destiny.'

Lorenzo nodded.

'And you fell in love with Rome?'

'Completely. When the first consul left, I stayed on with the new one. There's no handbook for being both mother and father. His father still reaches out from Ecuador. I let them have a relationship—it's complicated, but necessary.'

'For Miguel's sake,' he said with understanding.

'Yes. And we visit Ecuador annually. Miguel adores his grandfather's stories about our heritage.' Her eyes sparkled as she spoke of her son. 'But Rome … Rome has become our sanctuary.'

As she spoke about her time in Rome, there were moments when her narrative seemed to skirt around certain details. Her eyes drifted momentarily, as if weighing how much to reveal, before refocusing on Lorenzo with a practised smile.

Lorenzo shared memories of his Neapolitan upbringing, the vivid culture, and the close-knit community. As they traded stories, their connection deepened.

As a group spoke animatedly in Spanish, Camila's eyes scanned the room before returning to Lorenzo with a cautious smile. Her fingers traced a small scar on her wrist.

'Everything alright?' he asked, catching the fleeting change in her demeanour.

Her smile returned—warm but carefully controlled. 'Perfect. Just enjoying the music… I was thinking about something.'

A tinge of sadness in her eyes.

'You study the art like him too,' Camila said softly. 'My father. The same intensity, as if each brushstroke might whisper a secret.'

'And what secrets do you see?' Lorenzo asked, noticing how she angled herself to keep the door in sight.

She smiled, but something flickered in her eyes—too quick to name. 'That beauty and danger often wear the same face. In art, as in life.' She traced the rim of her glass. 'Take — without the darkness, the light loses its power. One defines the other.'

The observation struck Lorenzo as both profound and somehow personal, though he couldn't say why. 'You sound like you're speaking from experience.'

'Perhaps.' She met his gaze directly. 'Don't we all carry our own shadows, *Signor* Moretti?'

The question hung between them, heavy with unspoken meaning. In a long time, Lorenzo was seen.

Her next question—direct and full of possibility—caught him off guard. When she repeated it in Spanish, he couldn't help but laugh.

His heart soared. He grasped her hands, and exclaimed with pure joy, 'Yes, I want to have dinner with you, tomorrow!'

***

The night pulsed around them as they returned to the dance floor, their bodies moving in perfect synchronisation. Every glance carried new meaning, and every touch sparked electricity. Their shared laughter and movements spoke of something deeper blossoming between them—a connection that transcended their different paths to this moment.

He marvelled at her grace, her strength, and the way she had transformed adversity into wisdom. As the music played on, their bodies drew closer, each dance step turning into a new page in their stories.

As they danced, Lorenzo noticed her eyes occasionally scanning the room, her smile slightly less spontaneous than those of the other guests. When a man near the bar spoke animatedly on his phone, she subtly tensed, her hand gripping Lorenzo's shoulder before relaxing.

**

The gentle knock at seven-thirty made Lorenzo's heart skip. Camila greeted him with a radiant smile and presented a bottle of wine when he opened the door. The atmosphere created by candlelight inside his apartment warmly embraced her as evening fell.

'The bookshelves and art pieces in your home show its beauty to me as they perfectly capture your essence.'

He took the wine and responded with appreciation before asking her if she wanted a glass.

The deep red liquid swirled in their glasses while they embraced the room's quiet intimacy under the faint glow of candlelight accompanied by soft music. Their casual greetings quickly transformed into something deeper because they both sensed that their evening together held unexpected importance beyond a simple meet-up.

'You seem different outside the Ecuadorian setting,' Lorenzo remarked, watching her study the paintings on the wall. 'More at ease, yet somehow more guarded.'

Camila smiled, running a finger along the rim of her glass. 'The world teaches us to carry different versions of ourselves, depending on who's watching. You must know that better than most.'

'A banker's performance is rehearsed,' he admitted. 'We measure our words, conceal our instincts, and build walls between who we are and what we must be.'

She turned toward him, amusement flickering in her gaze. 'And yet, here you are, letting a stranger into your home. Either the walls are not as strong as you think, or you don't consider me a stranger anymore.'

Lorenzo chuckled, swirling the wine in his glass. 'Perhaps both. But tell me—how many versions of yourself have you had to become?'

She exhaled softly, as though weighing how much to reveal. 'Too many. I have been a daughter of privilege and a woman with nothing. I have been a wife, then a survivor. I have been a foreigner learning a new language, a mother building a life from scratch, and a professional navigating a world that was not designed for people like me.'

He leaned forward slightly. 'And now?'

She tilted her head, considering his question. 'Now, I am someone who refuses to be defined by circumstance alone. The world demands labels, but I reject the idea that I must be one thing or another. I exist in the in-between spaces—between countries, between expectations, between what is seen and what remains unsaid.'

Her words resonated with him more than he cared to admit. 'And yet, you speak as if that uncertainty is a choice. Most people fear living between definitions.'

Camila took a slow sip of wine, her gaze steady. 'Fear is the price of freedom. You can let it paralyse you, or you can let it sharpen you.'

A quiet understanding passed between them. They were both people who had, in their own ways, rewritten their fates.

Lorenzo refilled their glasses, allowing the silence to settle for a moment before asking, 'And Miguel? He must be the one constant in all this change.'

Her expression softened instantly. 'He is. He's my anchor, my purpose.' She paused, tracing the stem of her glass. 'But I never wanted him to inherit the weight of my choices. I want him to belong—to this city, to his own dreams—not to my struggles.'

Lorenzo nodded, understanding far more than he let on. 'Belonging is a strange thing. We regard it as a place, a home; however, at times, inside the places we construct, we are still like outsiders.'

'Yes,' she murmured, watching the candle flame flicker. 'And sometimes the places we belong to no longer exist, except in memory.'

The melancholy in her voice lingered between them. He had never known exile, not in the way she had, but he understood the way nostalgia could turn into something heavier—a ghost of what once was, lingering just out of reach.

'If you could go back to Ecuador tomorrow,' he asked suddenly, 'would you?'

She hesitated, then shook her head. 'No. I love my country, but my life is here now. My son's future is here.' She smiled, but there was something wistful in it. 'Besides, going back would mean reckoning with too many ghosts.'

Lorenzo studied her carefully. 'You mean Miguel's father?'

Camila's gaze didn't waver, but her fingers tightened around the stem of her glass. 'Among other things.'

For a moment, he considered pushing further, but he recognised that boundary—one he himself had often drawn when people ventured too close to his past. Instead, he shifted the conversation.

'So tell me,' he said, setting his glass down. 'What would you have been, in another life? If duty and survival had not dictated your path?'

She let out a quiet laugh, leaning back against the couch. 'An artist, maybe. Or a historian. Something that allowed me to live among stories, to make sense of them. And you?'

'A curator, perhaps,' he admitted. 'I always loved art, but I followed the path of security. Numbers, balance sheets, order. It seemed safer.'

'But safe is not the same as fulfilled.'

Her words were a gentle challenge, and he let himself acknowledge their truth.

Their conversation wove through philosophy, history, and the strange beauty of fate. The night stretched on, punctuated by laughter and moments of quiet contemplation. It was not flirtation in the usual sense—it was something deeper, a rare exchange of minds in a world that too often settled for surface connections.

At some point, Camila glanced at the time and sighed. 'I should go. Miguel will be home soon.'

Lorenzo stood, feeling the strange weight of parting even after just a few hours. He walked her to the door, hesitating before opening it.

'Tonight felt … different.' The words left his lips before he could second-guess them.

She met his gaze, searching for something. 'Yes, it did.'

For a moment, it seemed as though she might reach for

him, might lean into the tension that hung between them. But instead, she smiled—genuine, warm, leaving something unspoken but understood.

'Goodnight, Lorenzo.'

He watched as she disappeared into the quiet Rome night, leaving behind the lingering scent of her perfume and the weight of a conversation he knew he would replay in his mind long after she was gone.

***

Later, alone, he stared at the wine glass she'd used, the subtle curve of the rim catching the light, a silent echo of her presence. The room was no longer empty, yet it held the unmistakable presence of something unfinished.

His phone alerted him with a message.

Thank you for a beautiful evening. Sweet dreams.

He smiled in the darkness, already anticipating their next meeting.

His fingers hovered over the keyboard before he typed his reply:

Sweet dreams, Camila. Until next time.

CHAPTER 3

Lorenzo had spent the night in restless thought, the weight of the past week pressing down on him. The dinner with Camila, the flickers of hope in Miguel's eyes, even the brief moments of warmth at the party in Rocca Priora—they all seemed like distant memories now.

By the time dawn broke over Rome, he had convinced himself that his unease was nothing more than paranoia. He was wrong.

Stepping into his office that morning, something was unusual. The air was charged, heavy with a charged quietness between them.

At first, he dismissed it. Too little sleep. Too much stress.

Then, he noticed the small details—the way his assistant hesitated before greeting him, the brief pauses in whispered conversations as he passed. At the coffee machine, a conversation abruptly stopped. A colleague who usually greeted him warmly barely nodded before turning away.

Something was off.

He exhaled and settled into his chair, flipping through the morning reports. Focus. Routine. Keep moving.

The first email was routine. The second, a finance update.

The third—his breath caught.

Formal Investigation Notification—HR Department

The words blurred for a moment before refocusing. He read it again.

A formal complaint had been filed against him.

Inappropriate behaviour.

The phrase hung in the air, absurd and unfounded, yet coldly official.

Who?

His mind raced.

He scrolled down. A meeting with HR at noon. A few hours to figure out what this meant—not just in theory, but in consequence.

He busied himself with paperwork, but his attention drifted.

He kept rereading the HR email. The words seemed foreign, their weight unreal.

Inappropriate behaviour. Formal investigation.

The clinical phrasing on the page seemed to mock him, each carefully chosen word a hollow echo that did little to fill the gaping void of understanding.

Marina had never shown discomfort. Never hesitated in their conversations. Never once hinted at tension between them.

He picked up his phone and dialled her number.

Three rings. Four. Voicemail.

He tried again. This time, straight to voicemail.

Something was wrong.

Frowning, he switched to a text.

Marina, I just got an HR notification. Call me.

No reply.

His pulse quickened. He checked the bank's internal system. Offline.

His jaw tightened. Marina never went offline during work hours.

Rising abruptly, he crossed the floor to her desk. Empty. No coat, no coffee cup. Just a perfectly arranged workspace, as if she hadn't been there at all.

A colleague glanced up as he hovered nearby.

'Marina's not in?' he asked, keeping his voice casual.

The young analyst hesitated. 'She, uh … left early the day of the board meeting. Said she wasn't feeling well.'

Lorenzo nodded, thanked him, then walked back to his office. But his mind was racing.

She left before filing the complaint?

His phone was still in his hand. He tried calling her again. Straight to voicemail.

Not just the complaint. Not just the silence.

The timing. The precision.

Whoever had set this in motion had planned every step.

His eyes fell on the Trastevere loan files still open on his desk. Numbers that refused to sit right. A signature missing a timestamp.

43

A slow, uneasy realisation settled over him.

Marina hadn't just accused him.

She had disappeared.

And whoever was pulling the strings had already moved on to the next step.

***

The office was sterile, its white walls devoid of warmth. The HR director, a woman with sharp, impassive features, folded her hands neatly as Lorenzo took his seat.

'This is not an accusation,' she said, tone even. 'It's a process. The bank has a duty to investigate any concerns that arise.'

He nodded, keeping his expression unreadable. 'I understand. What exactly am I being accused of?'

'A junior colleague reported discomfort due to inappropriate behaviour during an offsite meeting.'

He exhaled sharply. 'I assume I have the right to know the specifics?'

'The details will be reviewed during the course of the inquiry.'

He studied her, reading the careful neutrality in her stance. This was already decided.

'Is this an official suspension?'

'Not at this stage. However, we advise against engaging with the complainant until the review is complete.'

He nearly laughed. It clearly was Marina accusing him and she wasn't even here.

That told him everything he needed to know.

Lorenzo barely had time to return to his office when an IT representative arrived, carrying a company-issued tablet. As he handed over his devices for the investigation, a sense of foreboding settled over him. This was no longer an internal review; it was a takedown.

He watched as the IT rep packed away his phone and laptop, each item sealed in a numbered evidence bag. The Trastevere files, work emails, and personal correspondence had been safely uploaded to an encrypted drive, a precaution he'd learned from a thriller: *Back up everything. Always.*

***

Lorenzo hesitated outside the unassuming office near Piazza Vittorio. The brass plaque reading *Studio Legale Camilleri* gleamed faintly under the dim streetlights.

Rosa had spoken highly of him—'A good lawyer, someone who knows how to help people like us.'

But Lorenzo couldn't shake his reservations.

He entered without an appointment.

Behind his disorganised desk with rolled sleeves Luigi Camilleri studied a case file while his thick glasses rested low on his nose. The office contained stacks of paper and antique legal books and a thin cloud of cigarette smoke lingered above.

Without looking up, Camilleri motioned for him to sit.

'So, Rosa finally sent you my way.'

Lorenzo studied him—dishevelled, with ill-fitting dentures and a Sicilian accent thick enough to belong in a 1950s courtroom drama. He was far from the polished legal minds Lorenzo had worked with in banking.

'I've been accused of inappropriate conduct at the bank,' he said finally.

Camilleri nodded as if he'd heard it all before.

'And you're telling me you did nothing improper.'

'I didn't.'

Camilleri picked up a pen and tapped it against the desk.

'Doesn't matter. What matters is who benefits from this accusation. Somebody wanted you out of the way.'

**

The Trastevere market buzzed with activity while the aroma of freshly baked bread blended with espresso notes filled the space. Lorenzo walked beside Camila and Miguel, their conversation light, their pace unhurried.

The weight of the investigation receded, replaced by something simpler.

Miguel tugged at his sleeve.

'Are you going to help me pick out the best gelato?'

Lorenzo smirked.

'Best in Rome? That's a serious challenge.'

Camila watched them, amusement flickering in her eyes.

'He takes gelato very seriously, you know.'

Lorenzo met her gaze, something unspoken passing between them.

If only things could stay this easy.

***

They strolled through the winding alleys, stopping at a small *gelateria* tucked between historic buildings. Miguel carefully examined the flavours, deep in contemplation.

'*Cioccolato* or *stracciatella*?' he asked, looking up at Lorenzo.

Lorenzo crouched beside him.

'You don't have to choose. Get both.'

Miguel's face lit up, and Camila laughed, shaking her head.

'You're a bad influence.'

Lorenzo only smiled, but beneath it, something gnawed at him.

He experienced this moment as if it belonged to a life that wasn't his destiny.

As they strolled next to the Tiber during the evening twilight and the day's light retreated beyond the city domes Camila cast a brief look at him before her forehead showed a slight crease.

'You've been quiet today.'

Lorenzo slowed his steps, weighing the moment. The words stayed on his tongue waiting to be spoken until he realised they were irreversible once he said them.

Tell her.

'My meeting with HR was today,' he finally revealed.

She continued to walk without interruption but he noticed a quick change in her body language along with an intensified concentration.

Camila kept her gaze on the river.

'About?'

He hesitated, then exhaled.

'A formal complaint. They're investigating me for misconduct.'

She didn't react immediately. When she finally spoke, her voice was unreadable.

'From whom?'

'Marina, one of my subordinates.'

Camila turned to face him then, studying his expression.

'Do you think it's connected to the bank files?'

The question hit harder than he expected. Because she didn't ask if he did it. She asked what it meant.

'I don't know yet,' he admitted.

After scrutinising him for an extended period she gave him a confirming nod.

'Then let's have another day like this.'

Lorenzo frowned.

'What do you mean?'

Her hand firmly yet tenderly enclosed his before she spoke.

'Let's go to Tuscany together.'

***

Two days later, the landscape outside the car window blurred into golden fields and distant hills, the familiar weight of Rome fading behind them.

Lorenzo let out his breath while he observed Camila as she

leaned back in her seat with her eyes shut and a gentle smile touching her lips.

'What?' she whispered without opening her eyes.

'Nothing,' he said, looking away.

Something about it gnawed at him.

For the first time in ages, silence didn't feel empty.

The hills of Montalcino rolled endlessly, golden under the autumn sun. The vineyards extended to the distant horizon with their hues transitioning between emerald and copper in a landscape free from any sense of urgency.

Lorenzo maintained a firm grip on the leather steering wheel while navigating the narrow roads. The concept of an impromptu adventure had long been forgotten until this moment when he stepped away from his obligations to enjoy the freedom.

By his side Camila opened the window so the warm breeze could touch her face. Her fingertips glided slowly across the edge of her sunglasses while she absorbed the scenery around her.

'You seem like someone who wouldn't choose to flee.'

He smirked.

'Who said I was running?'

'You took the first train out of Rome the moment I suggested it,' referring to a sudden trip to Naples for some unknown reasons.

He didn't answer, but she was right.

They stopped at a small, family run vineyard just outside Pienza.

The old man who owned the place with his weathered hands served them a glass of Rosso di Montalcino whose deep red colour captured the fading daylight.

With her eyes closed, Camila swirled the wine, the rich aroma filling her senses before she took a taste.

With a chuckle and a raised eyebrow Lorenzo responded. 'That's quite romantic.'

He observed her innate ability to merge flawlessly with her surroundings. The way she navigated life with ease while appreciating everything left him unsettled.

She abruptly set down her glass and asked him to share something new because when she questioned him about what his profession would be if he wasn't a banker he mentioned he would be an art curator.

He hesitated.

'I never gave it much thought beyond saying it.'

'You've dedicated so much time to building your life without ever questioning if this was truly what you desired.'

Her words settled between them, heavy but not unwelcome.

After many years, the same question echoed in his mind, a familiar refrain in the symphony of his thoughts.

***

By the time they arrived in Florence, the city had already begun to glow.

The Arno River mirrored the golden illumination from the Ponte Vecchio while quiet activity filled the streets.

They strolled through the Piazza della Signoria while tourists admired sculptures beside them and street musicians created soft melodies as old couples walked hand in hand.

Lorenzo barely noticed any of it. His entire concentration remained fixed solely on Camila.

The city's smells – exhaust fumes and roasting coffee—mingled in the air as she walked with him, her eyes tracing the buildings with a knowing affection.

She paused before the window of a tiny store where her reflection mingled with a messy pile of old books displayed behind the glass.

She faced him and asked, 'do you ever think about fate?'

'Not in the way most people do.'

'Then how?'

He paused for quite some time before responding to her question.

'Things happen. We assign them the weight we feel is appropriate. When we lack understanding of events, we resort to saying "stuff happens for a reason".'

She smiled slightly.

'That's very logical.'

'You disapprove?'

'No.' She turned back to the window. 'I just think some things are meant to happen, whether we fight them or not.'

He didn't ask what she meant.

He already knew.

***

The hotel, a weathered villa perched at Florence's edge, had walls that seemed to hum with the echoes of ages past; the very stones felt ancient beneath their fingertips.

From the balcony, Lorenzo observed the sprawling city below, a symphony of car horns and distant sirens weaving through the warm night air, as Camila lounged on the bed edge, the cool glass in her hand a contrast to the warmth of her skin.

He had spent years mastering risk. Calculating outcomes. Ensuring control. Yet here, in Florence, beneath the ancient streets and soft lamplight, the weight of his worries seemed to lift as the gentle sounds of the city lulled him. He didn't need an answer. Not yet.

'What are we doing, Lorenzo?' she asked quietly.

He turned, his eyes meeting hers. 'Spending time together.'

Though her lips curved into a smile, her eyes betrayed her, remaining flat and unaffected.

He walked across the room and stopped right in front of her. 'No.'

With trembling fingers, she mapped the line of his jaw, the warmth of his skin a stark contrast to the chill of her fear as she admitted her worry about becoming a crisis mistake.

'You're not.'

And he meant it.

The kiss was slow, a conversation without words. There was no urgency, no desperation—just the simple act of choosing this, choosing each other.

Later, as the city hummed in the distance and the night wrapped around them, Lorenzo traced his fingers along her bare shoulder, memorising the way she fit against him.

For a rare moment, he allowed himself to just be for what came next. He had Florence, the fading light, and the warmth of her hand in his. And for now, that was enough.

Florence glowed in the evening light, its beauty drawn from the contrast of light and shadow. Just like the art he loved. Just like the life he was finally willing to embrace.

***

By the time they returned to Rome, reality had already begun to creep back in.

Lorenzo unpacked slowly, letting the weight of responsibility settle back onto his shoulders.

Then, his phone buzzed.

'New developments in your case. Meeting required.'

He read the message twice.

The warmth of Tuscany faded, replaced by the cold certainty that whoever was behind this had made their next move.

He set his phone down, inhaled deeply, and reached for his jacket.

If they were expecting him to walk into this unprepared, they were wrong.

CHAPTER 4

A change was noticeable in the familiar conference room today. Lorenzo sat across from Giorgio and Paola, the bank's counsel, as they presented their findings.

'The investigation of Marina's devices revealed everything,' Giorgio began. 'The threatening emails came from her phone. She created a copy of your address and gathered information about you for months. The police managed to get all the information she didn't release directly from her service provider. We still don't know her whereabouts. Through our internal investigations among colleagues, we've built up a story that revealed her calculated scheme—she was deeply in debt and saw your position as her escape route. Your rejection of her advances pushed her over the edge.'

Lorenzo sat stunned. He'd known she had accused him falsely, but the background of her premeditated betrayal was staggering. Even more surprised about the advances that he hadn't noticed.

'We want to make this right,' Paola interjected. 'Full reinstatement, substantial compensation—'

'What about finding Marina?' Lorenzo cut in.

'Shouldn't that be the priority?'

Giorgio and Paola exchanged uncomfortable glances. 'The authorities are handling her disappearance,' Giorgio assured him. 'But your situation—'

'No.' Lorenzo's voice was firm. 'I can't accept any offers while she's missing under such suspicious circumstances. Discovering her fate is more important than financial settlement.'

Paola excused herself leaving the room.

Giorgio slid the file across the desk, the weight of it heavier than it should have been.

'Take it, Lorenzo. You get your life back. We all move forward.'

Lorenzo didn't touch it. 'And if I don't?'

Giorgio leaned back, his fingers drumming lightly against the desk.

'Then you become the story instead of the footnote.' A pause, then the smallest of smirks. 'And we both know who gets to write the ending.'

***

The days that followed brought no answers. Lorenzo compulsively checked his phone for updates, sleep eluding him. When exhaustion finally claimed him, Marina haunted his dreams—her once-friendly smile now masked with deception.

Camila watched with growing concern as shadows deepened under his eyes.

'*Mi amor,*' she would say, 'focus on what we have—our family, our love.'

But she knew he wouldn't rest until the truth emerged.

Then came that Saturday evening. Lorenzo's phone rang—

Giorgio's voice carried a weight that sent shivers down his spine.

'Come to the bank immediately. The police are here. It's about Marina.'

His hands trembled as he grabbed his keys. A tremor ran through him as he gripped the steering wheel, racing to the bank through Rome's darkened streets. Three grim faces awaited him in the conference room—Giorgio, a police investigator, and Luigi.

***

After weeks of searching, the investigator's clinical tone couldn't soften the horror: two boys playing in a field had discovered a suitcase containing Marina's body. The killer had brutally murdered her and disfigured her face. The police believed she had known her killer, had gone willingly to that remote spot where she met her end.

He didn't remember unlocking the door—only the moment his knees buckled. His breath came sharp, fractured, like something inside him had cracked along with Marina's life.

Camila's arms were around him before he registered her presence, her warmth pressing against the cold that had settled in his bones.

'This evil wasn't your doing, *mi amor*,' she murmured. 'We'll get through this.'

He nodded, but the words felt weightless. Marina had been many things—a colleague, a betrayer, a puzzle he never fully solved. But in the end, she was exactly what the bank made her—a name on a ledger, erased when the numbers stopped adding up.

As exhaustion pulled him under, a single thought remained: He hadn't saved her. And now, someone was making sure he wouldn't save himself either.

Though despair loomed, Lorenzo found a spark of resolve within himself. For too long, he played by the rules, neglecting the signs of corruption in his perfectly crafted world. Though tragic and senseless, Marina's death revealed the true price of his complacency. The past was unchangeable, and he was powerless to reverse what had happened. A renewed sense of purpose settled over Lorenzo as he resolutely returned to the files, his jaw clenched. He would see this through to the end, no matter the cost.

***

A month later, Lorenzo sat rigidly in Giorgio's office as his world tilted again.

'Marina was embezzling funds,' Giorgio announced, placing a document on the desk. 'Over a million euros through fraudulent loans. By making use of this.'

He stared at the document on the desk. His signature. His handwriting.

But it wasn't his.

The strokes were perfect, each curve of ink capturing the rhythm of his usual motion—almost too perfectly. This wasn't just a forgery. It was a painting, an imitation so precise that only an artist who had studied him intimately could have achieved it.

Lorenzo exhaled, his fingers tracing the edge of the page. A good forgery doesn't just mimic reality—it replaces it. And if it's perfect enough, it leaves no room for doubt.

They hadn't simply signed his name; they had reconstructed his presence, made him complicit in crimes he hadn't committed. Caught between light and shadow, truth was elusive, the most dangerous lies were not those in the shadows, but those that stood fully in the light.

His mind drifted back to Caravaggio's works—the saints emerging from darkness, their faces half-lit, caught between damnation and redemption. What if the truth was never a matter of exposure, but of perspective? What if stepping into the light didn't reveal, but only distorted?

His heartbeat sped up. Giorgio's signature. The one Marina had shown him weeks ago—the one that had made him doubt everything. He had taken it at face value, had assumed Giorgio had signed off on those irregular loans, just as he was now expected to believe he had done the same. But looking at this —his own forged name, replicated with surgical accuracy—a gnawing certainty overcame him.

There was more to this than met the eye.

Had Marina known? Or worse—had she orchestrated it? The way she had guided him back then, the way she had framed the evidence so neatly—it all came rushing back, sharp and insidious. She hadn't just placed doubts in his mind; she had built the entire narrative. She had made him see Giorgio as the problem, just as someone was now ensuring he would be next.

It dawned on him, slow but undeniable like a slow, creeping shadow.

This wasn't just fraud. This was manipulation at the highest level. And this time, he wouldn't be a spectator to his own downfall.

And, he had been playing right into it.

'We need to investigate these signatures thoroughly before making any decisions. I'm sure you understand that we need to search further, and... the reinstatement offer is off the table until the police excludes you from any wrongdoings.' Giorgio's voice was heavy.

'You can't believe I was involved!'

'I don't. But the board wants this contained, truth be damned.'

***

That evening, Lorenzo barely touched his dinner as he explained to Camila.

'We fight,' she said firmly, eyes flashing. 'You won't be their scapegoat.'

Luigi agreed when they met the next day. 'The situation is complex, but we can challenge them.'

Then the letters arrived. First, an *avviso di garanzia*—he was under investigation for embezzlement. Second, a police summons about Marina's murder. As Lorenzo read them, memories of his former colleague's recent behaviour took on sinister new meaning.

***

Lorenzo, accompanied by Luigi, found Inspector Albanese's office oppressive. The detective's eyes were sharp behind his desk.

'Sit, *Dottor* Moretti. Let's discuss your relationship with Marina Ricci.'

He explained their relationship was purely professional until her recent attempts at friendship. He noticed Albanese's interest sharpen.

'When exactly did she become more… friendly?'

'During her last days at the office. She started suggesting coffee and lunch.'

'And you never found this change suspicious?'

'I thought she was just being collegial.' His voice tightened. 'Now I wonder if she was trying to divert attention from her crimes.'

'Or making you the scapegoat,' the inspector mused. 'But then someone killed her. Rather inconvenient timing, wouldn't you say?'

The implication hung heavy in the air. Lorenzo met the inspector's gaze steadily.

'I had nothing to do with her death. But you're right—the timing is suspicious. Almost as if someone wanted to silence her.'

The interview dragged on as Albanese probed his history with Marina from every angle. Lorenzo answered as best he could, hoping his forthrightness would convince the inspector of his innocence.

Finally, after hours, Albanese closed the file and peered at him intently.

'You say you have no idea who could have wanted *Signora* Ricci dead. No grudges, vendettas, angry lovers?'

Lorenzo shook his head helplessly.

'She never mentioned anything. But her embezzlement must have made enemies. Maybe it was... retribution?'

He hated voicing the dark possibility.

Albanese observed him for a long moment.

'Two investigations now, *Signor* Moretti. Embezzlement and murder. Keep yourself available.'

***

Walking home, Lorenzo's mind raced. The Trastevere loan patterns he'd first noticed now seemed like merely the surface of something far more sinister. But who else was involved? Who had wanted her dead? And how could he prove his innocence?

Paolo, a bank senior accountant he'd once mentored, proved willing to help.

'I never believed all those accusations,' he said. Together, they combed through Marina's digital footprint, searching for connections.

The breakthrough came in exchanges between Marina and Lucio Giancarlo, a senior officer from risk management, via an internal communication tool hidden in a private channel. Their coded messages hinted at deeper collaboration, but Lorenzo needed more.

Then came the notebook.

A small leather-bound volume arrived at his apartment by courier, anonymous envelope, no return address. His fingers trembled as he photographed pages filled with transactions and the initials *LG* scattered throughout. The Trastevere loans were there, but they led to something bigger—Phoenix Corp.

***

That evening, he spread the evidence before Camila, his excitement palpable. 'Look—proof of their connection! I'm getting closer.'

But Camila's eyes held worry, not triumph.

'Lorenzo,' she said gently, 'this obsession is consuming you. Maybe it's time to let the police handle it.'

'It's not enough yet,' he insisted. 'I need irrefutable proof.'

'And what about us?'

Her voice cracked.

'What about Miguel? We hardly see you anymore.'

He really looked at her then, saw the exhaustion in her posture and the dimmed light in her eyes. Guilt twisted in his chest.

'You've both sacrificed so much already,' he acknowledged.

'I need time to focus on Miguel,' she said softly. 'He needs his mother back. And you need space from this darkness clouding your mind.'

Though it pained him, he knew she spoke truth. His quest had blinded him to what mattered most.

'Take whatever time you need with your son,' he said, taking her hands. 'I'll be here when you're ready.'

But even as he held her, his mind raced with new connections. Phoenix Corp was registered to Silvio Bianchi. Why was bank money flowing to his business? The Trastevere loans seemed to be just one part of a larger scheme.

***

Late one night, Lorenzo stared at Miguel's drawing on his refrigerator—a family portrait from happier days. The boy's crayon figures smiled broadly, hands linked together. When had he last spent an evening just playing with the boy, listening to his stories?

His phone buzzed—another lead about Phoenix Corp. His hand hovered over it, remembering Camila's words about obsession. The truth was within reach, but it was costing him everything that mattered.

'Papà?' Miguel's voice from a week ago echoed in his memory. 'When are you coming to play with me again?'

The moment the child's voice cracked with loneliness, he knew he had to trust the authorities. No case was worth sacrificing his family again. He set the phone down. Some truths, he realised, came at too high a price.

***

The next morning brought something worse.

Inside his mailbox lay a plain white envelope, his name printed in stark block letters. The message inside was a cartography of threat, mapped in a language that straddled borders:

Señor Moretti, Su investigation threatens more than institutions. It unravels threads woven across continents, sangre, and memory. Each question you ask casts a shadow longer than you comprehend. Détente ahora, or the consequences will consume everything you've dared to love. This is not a warning. This is a prophecy.

The message bore no signature—only a watermark of a phoenix, rising and falling, a symbol of destruction and rebirth.

The letter fluttered from his trembling hands. Someone threatened to harm Camila and Miguel if he continued investigating Marina's crimes. He scanned the quiet street but saw only neighbours starting their day, oblivious to how his world had just tilted.

His first call was to Rosa.

'I need your help,' Lorenzo said, his voice low despite being alone in his office. 'Camila and Miguel—they're in danger.'

'*Dios mío.*' Rosa's voice crackled through the phone. A pause, then: 'My cousin's husband works security at the consulate. He mentioned… concerns. But I didn't want to believe—'

'What kind of concerns?' Lorenzo interrupted, suddenly sharp. 'Rosa, how long have you known something was wrong?'

'When you work in people's homes for twenty years, you learn to listen. To watch.'

Her voice dropped lower.

'The cleaning lady at the consulate, she's my friend from church. Last week she told me someone was shredding documents after hours. They had your bank logo on them—'

Lorenzo gripped the phone tighter, his mind racing. Rosa's network wasn't mystical after all—just the invisible web of service workers that kept Rome running, eyes and ears everywhere, connected by shared hopes and common roots.

'Can you talk to Camila? Convince her they need to leave town temporarily?'

His voice faltered. 'She's already pulled away because of my obsession with the case. But now...'

'Of course, *mijo*.' Rosa's voice grew steely with resolve. 'I will speak with her. And I will ask around our community—perhaps someone has heard whispers about these threats.'

After hanging up, he paced his apartment. He paused at the window, watching a dark sedan drive past for the third time that morning. Camila's gentle smile and Miguel's laughter haunted him. He would die before letting harm come to them. But could he abandon the investigation when he was so close to exposing the truth?

His eyes fell on the photo from their Tuscan holiday—Camila and Miguel laughing as pigeons scattered around them in Siena's square. The joy in their faces pierced his heart. Next to it lay the files about Trastevere, the notebook's cryptic numbers, all the evidence pointing to something much darker than simple loan fraud.

He picked up the threatening letter again, studying the awkward

Spanish phrasing. Someone wanted him scared, wanted him to back off. The mention of *sangre*—blood—felt too deliberate, too personal. Like the writer knew about Camila's Ecuadorian connections.

No, he couldn't stop completely. But he could be smarter. More careful. The Trastevere investigation had started with official bank documents; perhaps there were other legal routes he hadn't explored.

First, though, he needed to wait. Rosa's steady wisdom and deep connections in the Ecuadorian community might uncover crucial information. Sometimes, the best path forward required a tactical retreat.

***

When Camila arrived, her eyes were already clouded with worry.

'Rosa said it was urgent?'

He handed her the threatening letter. He watched her face pale as she read, then transform with a fierce determination he recognised—the same look she'd had when confronting her son's kidnapper.

'You have to leave Rome,' he pleaded. 'Just until it's safe.'

'No.' Camila's voice was steel wrapped in silk. 'I won't let them chase us away while you remain in danger.'

'But Miguel—'

'Needs his father, too.' She took his hands in hers, her grip strong despite her trembling. 'We face this together, or not at all.'

He pulled her close, overwhelmed by her courage, even as his mind raced with possibilities. The Trastevere loans, Phoenix Corp, Marina's notebook—all the pieces were there. But now the stakes were infinitely higher.

***

Later that day, Rosa brought news that made his blood run cold.

'A name keeps coming up—Silvio Bianchi,' she whispered. 'He does the mob's dirty work. The kind that ends with bodies in suitcases. Be careful, Lorenzo.'

The web connecting Marina, Lucio, and the mafia was unravelling. But he needed more.

'Can you ask about Bianchi's operations?' he asked Rosa. 'I'll meet anyone, anywhere.'

Her hesitation spoke volumes.

'People are terrified of him. But I'll try.'

The weight of it all pressed down on him: the investigation, the threats, the lives at stake. But as he held Camila that evening, watching the sun set over Rome's ancient rooftops, he knew there would be no backing down. They would find a way through this—together.

She was right. Running wasn't the answer. But neither was reckless pursuit of the truth. There had to be a middle path, one that would keep his family safe while bringing justice to light.

For now, though, he had to think carefully about his next move.

***

His phone buzzed—Rosa had found someone willing to talk, tonight. Hope and dread mingled in his chest as he read the message.

'I have to meet this contact,' he told Camila, reaching for his coat.

She caught his hand. 'Promise me something first.'

'Anything.'

'No more lone crusades.' Her eyes held his.

Lorenzo nodded, drawing strength from her resolve.

He kissed her goodbye, hoping this meeting could change everything.

***

The small cantina in Caprarola stood alone against the darkened hills, its windows the only source of light for miles. Outside, the night smelled of damp earth and chestnut trees, the silence punctuated only by the distant hum of cicadas.

Lorenzo arrived early, selecting a seat that allowed him to watch both the entrance and the parking lot. He ran his fingers along the edge of his wine glass, his fingers steady despite the undercurrent of unease in his gut.

Twenty minutes later, the door chimed. A man in his forties entered, pausing at the threshold. His gaze swept the empty restaurant before settling on Lorenzo.

'*Hola*, Lorenzo.' His Spanish carried the clipped precision of someone who had lived between two languages for too long. '*Soy Carlos.*'

Lorenzo gestured to the chair opposite him. '*Gracias por venir.*'

Carlos settled in, taking his time to study the menu. He didn't speak until the waiter had brought water and stepped away. Only then did he remove his reading glasses and exhale, as if bracing himself.

'Has Rosa explained what I'm investigating?' Lorenzo prompted.

Carlos nodded, his expression tightening. '*Sí*. Silvio Bianchi… he wasn't always the monster you hear about now. At first, he was just another friend to our community. He learned our language, attended our gatherings. Then he married one of us—Mariana, an undocumented young woman.'

Lorenzo leaned forward. 'Married? But she was undocumented?'

'They wed in Cuenca and returned as husband and wife. It was common then—many of us had similar arrangements.'

Carlos's fingers traced the condensation on his glass, his voice lowering.

'Three years later, Mariana vanished. Bianchi claimed she returned to Ecuador, but when we searched…'

He shook his head.

'Her family in Cuenca never heard from her. Her brothers came to Italy and tried to file a police report, but …'

He spread his hands helplessly.

'Bianchi used her undocumented status against them. He made sure they had more to fear than he did.'

Lorenzo swallowed, a sick feeling creeping up his spine.

'Didn't they try to fight back?'

'They threatened him, but he retaliated, accusing Mariana of fleeing with a million euros of his money.'

'And after that?' Lorenzo asked quietly.

Carlos let out a slow breath.

'Bianchi changed. He began offering "help"—money, jobs, favours. To outsiders, he was still a generous benefactor. But within our community…'

His voice dropped to a whisper.

'The loans he gave so freely came with impossible demands. Pay immediately, or pay with your life.'

Lorenzo's grip on his glass tightened.

'How many people?'

'At least fifteen,' Carlos said. 'I found out through a friend—Manolo. One night, he was desperate, drunk, telling me he owed Bianchi thirty thousand euros. That money had gone straight to his family in Santo Domingo, to buy a house for his wife and children.'

The main course arrived—*ravioli alla castagna*—but neither of them touched their plates. The wine flowed quickly, as if trying to drown the weight of the conversation.

Carlos leaned forward, his voice low.

'One day, a woman approached Manolo outside Phoenix Corp. She looked professional, but something was wrong.'

Lorenzo's pulse quickened. 'Who?'

Carlos met his eyes. 'Marina.'

The name hit like a slap.

'Are you sure?' Lorenzo asked.

Carlos nodded grimly.

'She offered him a loan—forty-three thousand euros at an impossibly low rate. The catch? Ten thousand had to go to her "facilitators."'

Lorenzo exhaled sharply.

'And Manolo accepted?'

'Three weeks later, the money appeared in his account. Thirty thousand went straight to Bianchi, the rest to Marina's contacts.'

Carlos took a sip of wine.

'We thought Bianchi was finished after that. Until—'

'Until what?'

Carlos hesitated.

'One night in Trastevere, I saw them together. Marina and Bianchi. They looked… comfortable. That's when we knew—they'd been working together all along.'

The weight of the revelation pressed down on Lorenzo. Marina had arranged the loans, taking a cut for herself and Bianchi, all while keeping up the pretence of a mere banker caught in the wrong place at the wrong time. The forged signatures, the loans, the connection to Phoenix Corp—it was an elegant scheme.

Until something had gone terribly wrong.

Carlos pulled on his coat.

'Whatever you find, be careful. Bianchi has eyes everywhere.'

After Carlos left, Lorenzo remained seated, staring into his untouched plate.

Had Marina made a mistake? Had she crossed the wrong people? Or had she been eliminated for knowing too much?

As the night stretched on, only one thing became clear—whoever had killed Marina hadn't done it out of impulse.

It had been calculated.

And he was next.

***

Back to his apartment, Lorenzo paced, the evening's revelations churning in his mind. The empty Rosso di Montalcino bottle sat on his counter, a reminder of happier times planned with Camila.

He pulled out his phone, thumb hovering over her unanswered messages.

CHAPTER 5

The jumble of papers on Lorenzo's desk seemed to mock him as his mind raced while he desperately searched through the scattered documents and files. Each piece of evidence he uncovered felt like a blow to his carefully constructed reality, each connection a tiny crack in the foundation of his life, letting in the cold, harsh light of truth.

The familiar, dark wood of his study pressed in on him, the silence broken only by the frantic scratching of his pen as he struggled against the web of corruption and deceit that felt like an inescapable prison.

The harsh glare of the computer screen reflected in Lorenzo's tired eyes; the blinking cursor seemed to pulse with a malevolent energy. One wrong click, he knew, and the painstaking progress he'd made could crumble. He could almost smell the stale air of impending failure.

His cursor hovered over the police contact page, a moment of calculated hesitation. 'Not yet,' he muttered, closing the tab with a deliberate click.

'You're still at it?' Camila's voice carried both concern and a hint of resignation. She stood in the doorway, two steaming cups creating tendrils of aromatic steam—a peace offering, a lifeline.

'I need to be thorough before involving the authorities.' The words carried the weight of his obsessive precision.

Lorenzo accepted the coffee she offered, their fingers brushing—a momentary connection in his consuming investigation.

'*Mi amor,*' she set her cup down, placing her hands on his shoulders with a gentle firmness, 'Luigi said—'

'I know what Luigi said.' He covered her hand with his, a gesture both tender and protective. 'But corruption doesn't stay at the bottom, Camila. It rises like smoke.'

'And what if that smoke suffocates you first?'

Before she could elaborate, his phone buzzed—Luigi requesting an urgent meeting.

***

'You look terrible,' Luigi said as Lorenzo slid into the seat across from him, the wooden chair scraping against the tiled floor with a sound that seemed to cut through the café's stillness.

'Thanks for the compliment.'

Lorenzo's response carried a dry edge, masking the weight of his investigation.

'Lorenzo, this isn't a joke anymore. The threats—'

'Are exactly why I can't go to the police yet.' Lorenzo leaned forward, his voice low, intense. 'Think about it. How many officers do you think Bianchi has in his pocket?'

Luigi's frown deepened, etching lines of concern across his weathered face.

'And how many fingers do you think he'd break to keep you quiet? And that is if you are lucky.'

'As many as it takes. Which is why we need concrete evidence first.'

'We?'

The lawyer raised an eyebrow, a mix of scepticism and unexpected intrigue.

'Who else is involved?'

Lorenzo hesitated—a momentary crack in his carefully maintained composure.

'Paolo's been helping me dig through records.'

'*Dio mio*,' Luigi muttered. 'Who's this Paolo, now? You're both going to get yourselves bloody killed.'

***

'Look at this,' Paolo suddenly said, sliding a document across the desk, in the evening at Lorenzo's. His finger traced Giorgio's signature on loan approvals, each stroke revealing something more sinister than a mere administrative error.

Lorenzo studied the paper, his eyes narrowing.

'The patterns are getting clearer. See how the requirements were systematically ignored?'

'Not ignored,' Paolo corrected, pulling up more files with a precision that spoke of hours of meticulous work. 'Deliberately circumvented, thanks to Giorgio's new directives. Look at the dates—these all coincide with Marina's involvement.'

***

Lorenzo's phone buzzed—Camila checking in. A moment of personal connection piercing through his investigative obsession.

He realised he was falling into old habits—prioritising the mission over relationships, just as he had done with the Marina case. This time, he put down his work and called Camila.

'You should go,' Paolo said, reading the unspoken tension in the room. 'We've been at this for hours.'

'Just a bit longer. I think we're close to something.'

Lorenzo pulled up another document, his cursor moving with surgical precision.

'See this? The bank's lending standards didn't just relax—they were dismantled. And look who approved the changes.'

Paolo whistled low, a sound that carried more meaning than words.

'Giorgio's fingerprints are all over this.'

'Not that I had many doubts about it, but I gave him some slack,' he added.

'So,' Paolo interjected, 'Marina wasn't being entirely untrue about this.'

'Not at all. She even mentioned not to trust anyone, including her.'

Paolo gave a wry smile.

'But we need more than fingerprints. We need—'

Lorenzo stopped, something caught his eye on the screen.

'Paolo, look at this transaction pattern.'

The accountant moved closer, leaning over Lorenzo's shoulder. His eyes widened—a silent language of discovery.

'Mother of God...'

Paolo tapped the edge of a printout with his index finger, his voice low but insistent.

'Look at this, Lorenzo. Every transaction linked to that shell company routes through the same two intermediaries.'

He slid the document across the desk.

'Guess where their headquarters is?'

Lorenzo flipped through the files, his brows drawing together in concentration. His eyes locked onto a familiar address.

'Trastevere,' he murmured.

Then his frown deepened.

'And not just any office—this company was dissolved two years ago. Someone's using a dead firm to move money under the radar.'

'Exactly.'

Paolo leaned in, lowering his voice as he pointed to another set of documents.

'And the signatory? Marina. But look at the approval chain—her request should never have gone through without additional verification.'

Lorenzo exhaled sharply, running a hand through his hair.

'Unless someone inside the compliance team overrode it,' he said, his tone edged with certainty. 'This isn't just negligence. Someone was actively covering these transactions.'

Paolo's expression darkened as he pulled up another set of data.

'And the biggest red flag? These accounts—see the timestamps?'

He jabbed at a series of numbers.

'Transfers always happened late at night, right after market close. They were washing funds before morning trading.'

Lorenzo's jaw tightened. He shut the file and leaned back in his chair, staring at the ceiling for a moment before muttering,

'Damn it.'

He sat forward again, voice low but firm.

'This isn't just fraud—this is organised. Someone inside the bank has been feeding them information.'

'We need to make copies. Now.'

Lorenzo's fingers flew across the keyboard, each keystroke a potential blow against the corruption they were unravelling.

'It's what we've been looking for,' Paolo finished. 'The connection between Giorgio and Bianchi's operation.'

Lorenzo sat back, running a hand through his hair—a gesture that betrayed his underlying exhaustion.

'This is bigger than we thought, isn't it?'

'And more dangerous.' Paolo's voice was grim, weighted with unspoken implications.

'Are you sure you want to keep going?'

Lorenzo's mind flashed with images: immigrants trapped in endless debt cycles, Marina's body in that cold suitcase, Camila and Miguel's worried faces.

Fragments of a larger, more insidious narrative.

'We've come too far to stop now.'

Paolo nodded, determination hardening his features like tempered steel.

'Then let's make these bastards pay.'

They worked through the night, building their case piece by piece. The truth emerged—ugly, dangerous, but undeniable.

Lorenzo knew they were walking a tightrope, each document uncovered, each connection made bringing justice closer.

High expenses were possible; however, remaining silent would be far costlier.

***

Giovanni Sabelli's office was exactly what Lorenzo expected from a former police detective turned private investigator—sparse, practical, with case files neatly arranged on industrial shelves. A single photo of a smiling woman—presumably his wife—sat on the desk, a hint of humanity in an otherwise clinical space.

'Luigi Camilleri speaks highly of you,' Lorenzo said, settling into the chair across from Giovanni.

The leather creaked beneath him, a subtle counterpoint to the room's stillness.

The detective's weathered face remained neutral.

At sixty-three, his eyes still held the sharp intensity that had helped him crack countless organised crime cases—eyes that had seen more than most could imagine.

'Luigi mentioned you're in a dangerous situation.'

'Marina Ricci.'

Lorenzo moved nearer, his tone quiet and focused.

'I need to know everything about her.'

Giovanni's pen scratched against his notepad—a rhythmic sound that seemed to hold its own significance.

'The banker found in the suitcase. Why are you interested in her story?'

'Because she tried to frame me before she died.'

Giovanni's pen stopped. He studied Lorenzo thoughtfully, measuring something beyond the words spoken. Then, a single nod.

'Give me two weeks.'

When Lorenzo returned, Giovanni had a thick file waiting—its mere presence promising revelations.

***

'Your instincts were right. Marina Ricci's past is… complicated.'

'How so?'

'Born to wealth, but her family's money wasn't clean.'

Giovanni spread out several documents like a macabre puzzle.

'Mental health issues in her teens, substance abuse in her twenties. Yet somehow lands a prestigious position at your bank.'

Lorenzo frowned, the pieces not quite fitting.

'Family connections?'

'Partly. But there's more.'

Giovanni pulled out a photograph—a young Marina with a familiar face that chilled Lorenzo to the bone.

'Recognise him?'

'Silvio Bianchi.'

'Exactly. And here's where it gets interesting.'

Giovanni leaned back, the weight of knowledge pressing between them.

'She was using you, Lorenzo. Setting you up as a fall guy while another manager was already in their pocket.'

'Giorgio?'

'The police are looking at him closely. But you—' Giovanni held up a hand, '—are no longer a suspect in her murder.'

'Thank God for that.'

Lorenzo's listened attentively at Giovanni revealing more pieces of the puzzle. Giancarlo's involvement, Marina's cryptic—each new detail pointed to a web of corruption far deeper than he'd suspected.

As Giovanni handed over the photocopied pages, a conspiratorial gesture accompanied by a warning, Lorenzo felt a growing sense of unease. The notebook held secrets the police couldn't decipher, but with his banking knowledge, he might unravel the truth.

Leaning back in his chair, Lorenzo stared at the ceiling, a heavy realisation settling in his gut. Someone inside the bank was feeding information to criminal entities.

A barely suppressed fury shook him as he ground out, 'Damn it.'

***

'It's a code,' Paolo said later that evening, squinting at Marina's cramped handwriting.

They sat at his dining room table, the notebook spread between them alongside half-empty wine glasses—evidence of their long night of investigation.

'Look at these patterns,' Lorenzo pointed.

His finger traced the intricate web of dates, amounts, initials—each mark potentially a key to something larger.

Paolo stroked his hair in frustration, the gesture betraying their mounting tension.

'But what's the key? Without understanding their system '

'We need Giovanni.'

Lorenzo was already reaching for his phone, determination etched into every line of his face.

'He's spent decades cracking mafia codes. Let's tell him what we understood. It might help him.'

***

They found the detective at a local restaurant, tucked away in his usual corner—a man of habits, of predictable movements in an unpredictable world.

His eyebrows rose as they approached, a silent commentary on their unexpected visit.

'Twice in one day? Must be important, otherwise I start believing you are developing feelings for me.'

Lorenzo slid into the booth, Paolo following. The booth's vinyl upholstery creaked beneath their weight—a mundane sound against the gravity of their conversation.

'We need your expertise with the notebook. It's a code. We can't make much sense of it. We have managed to decrypt some data that you might find useful, but there's something we can't figure out.'

Giovanni studied several pages, his expression growing grave. Each passing moment seemed to add weight to the room, to the investigation.

'These patterns… I've seen similar methods used by certain families. Give me time with this.'

He looked up sharply, his gaze cutting through Lorenzo like a knife.

'But Lorenzo—watch your back. People have died for less than what's in these pages.'

As they left, a mixture of hope and dread washed over Lorenzo. Each answer only revealed more questions, more dangers. Paolo clapped him on the shoulder—a gesture of solidarity, of shared risk.

'We'll crack this, my friend.'

Lorenzo nodded, though his thoughts were already racing ahead to what other secrets Marina's notebook might reveal—and who might kill to keep those secrets hidden.

**

Camila watched Lorenzo hunched over Marina's notebook for the third straight night, his dinner going cold beside him—a forgotten offering to his growing obsession.

The dim desk lamp cast intricate shadows across his face, deepening the dark circles under his eyes like cartographic lines marking unexplored territories of exhaustion.

She placed a hand on his shoulder—a gesture both tender and desperate.

He barely seemed to notice, his concentration a fortress

impenetrable by simple human touch.

'Lorenzo?' she whispered.

'Hmm?'

He didn't look up from the cryptic pages, each line seeming to hold some fragment of a larger, more dangerous truth.

'Miguel asked why you missed his football match today.'

That made him pause. Guilt flickered across his features like a brief, painful shadow.

'I'm sorry, I completely forgot—'

'Like you forgot our dinner with Rosa last week? Or the embassy function?'

Her voice cracked, a delicate fissure revealing deeper fractures.

'You're here physically, *mi amor*, but not at all.'

He finally turned to face her, seeming to see her anew in days—truly see her.

'Camila, I—'

'No, let me finish.'

She took a steadying breath, her composure a fragile construct.

'I understand how important this investigation is. But I can't watch you disappear into it completely. Miguel and I... we need more than just your ghost.'

***

After getting Miguel off to school the following day, Camila found Lorenzo in the kitchen—a rare moment of physical presence that seemed almost unusual.

Sunlight spilled across the marble countertop, casting a soft warmth that seemed to contrast with the tension between them.

'We need to talk,' she said quietly, her words hanging in the air like a delicate glass ornament—beautiful, but capable of shattering at the slightest pressure.

He nodded, his expression already resigned, carrying the weight of impending loss.

'I think...' her fingers twisted together, a subtle dance of uncertainty.

'I think you shouldn't spend time here anymore. You have to go back to your apartment.'

'Camila—' The protest started automatically, a reflex born of habit.

'Please, let me explain. You need space to focus on your investigation. And I need...'

She swallowed hard, the words catching in her throat like a half-formed prayer.

'I need to end my sense that I'm competing with a notebook for your attention.'

He reached for her hand, a gesture of connection, but she stepped back—a choreographed movement of emotional distance.

'It's not forever,' she continued, her voice steady despite the tremor beneath. 'Just until this is over. Until you find your way back to us.'

'I never meant to hurt you,' he said softly, the words a gentle wound.

'I know. That's what makes it worse.'

***

The bar near Termini station hummed with pre-dinner energy, a cacophony of conversations and clinking glasses that seemed to fade into background noise as Lorenzo met Luigi.

His lawyer's expression was unusually bright, a stark contrast to the weight of their previous conversations.

'As I didn't manage to mention during our last meeting, the bank wants you back,' Luigi announced without preamble, his words cutting through the ambient noise like a sharp knife.

Lorenzo's coffee cup froze halfway to his lips, suspended between motion and stillness.

'Do they, really?'

'HR has evidence clearing you completely. They're offering your position back, with full back pay.'

'There has to be a catch.'

The lawyer nodded, a gesture that spoke volumes.

'They want you to take voluntary retirement immediately after reinstatement. Early retirement package, generous compensation—'

'A golden handshake to disappear quietly.'

'Lorenzo—' Luigi leaned forward, his voice dropping to a confidential tone. '—as your lawyer and friend, take the deal. Go travelling the world and follow your passion for arts. This amateur investigation of yours… you're poking a hornet's nest of organised crime. These people don't play by the rules.'

'But the corruption—'

'Will still be there whether you martyr yourself or not,' his voice softened, becoming an almost paternal whisper.

'You're already losing Camila. How much more are you willing to sacrifice?'

Lorenzo stared into his coffee, seeing Camila's tear-stained face, Miguel's disappointed eyes reflected in the dark liquid.

'When did you become so wise?'

'When I stopped trying to save the world and started trying to save what I could.'

Luigi checked his watch, the movement crisp and precise.

'My train leaves soon. Promise me you'll think about it?'

***

The apartment felt like a mausoleum of memories, the silence deafening after weeks of family sounds.

Only Rosa's meticulously tended plants showed any sign of life, their green leaves a stark contrast to the sterile emptiness.

The stillness of his study, broken only by the whisper of turning pages, drew him to a painting he had previously ignored—a small canvas showing a family gathered around a rustic table. The scene radiated a palpable sense of intimacy and shared warmth. It lacked Caravaggio's dramatic flair and Gentileschi's precision, yet a comforting essence emanated from the painting.

Finally, he understood its appeal—not every masterpiece was about grandeur. Sometimes, the beauty lay in the simplicity of human connection.

While reviewing his accumulated mail, he froze at an old newspaper headline.

The news of Marina's fate crystallised his decision—protecting his family meant choosing strategic retreat over reckless pursuit of justice.

He pondered Camila and Miguel, sheltered by diplomatic walls.

Perhaps it was time to let others carry this burden. Some battles weren't worth the cost of winning.

GRUESOME DISCOVERY IN REMOTE FIELD OUTSIDE ROME.

His hands quivered as he read the headline.

The espresso turned bitter in his mouth.

Two local boys made a ghastly discovery while playing in a remote field near the outskirts of Rome. Police reports indicated the children discovered a large, fastened suitcase partially buried by a cluster of trees.

He could picture it—children's curiosity turning to horror, innocence colliding with brutal reality.

The newspaper crinkled in his tightening grip, the sound sharp and brittle.

Investigators identified Marina Ricci, age 29, as the victim; she was last seen leaving the Rome headquarters of the bank where she worked. Despite her upstanding position, Ricci was associated with mobsters and underworld figures. Police suspected her death was a retaliatory mafia hit related to her involvement in organised crime activities.

'Christ, Marina,' he whispered, setting down his cup with a small, precise movement.

He remembered her first day at the bank—sharp, ambitious, with a smile that could charm anyone.

Was darkness present, though hidden?

The article detailed her troubled history—family turmoil, substance abuse, criminal ties. Clinical words that failed to capture the complexity of a life gone wrong.

He thought of their rare shared lunches and the easy rapport they'd built before everything unravelled.

How little he'd known her.

His eyes caught on the description of her body—*severely mutilated*.

The coffee threatened to come back up. Even after she'd tried to frame him, even after everything she'd done, nobody deserved such an end.

The article concluded that *citizens with information are urged to come forward. Investigators remain committed to bringing those responsible to justice.*

He set the paper aside, but the images wouldn't leave him—Marina's life reduced to forensic details, her complexity erased by brutal circumstance.

***

His phone buzzed—a message from Luigi about the bank's offer.

The timing seemed a sign, a cosmic punctuation to his internal struggle.

By the time this concludes, how many more bodies will be discovered in suitcases? How many more lives will the endless cycle of greed and revenge destroy?

Lorenzo stood, walking to the window. The morning sun flung long shadows across Rome's ancient streets—layers of history bearing silent witness to countless untold stories of corruption and loss.

Somewhere out there, Marina's killers walked free, while he sat here wrestling with his conscience.

But what good was martyrdom? What justice could one man achieve against a system built on decades of corruption?

He picked up his phone, typing a response to Luigi: *Let's discuss the terms.*

Perhaps there were better ways to fight darkness than charging blindly into it.

He looked again at Marina's article, left on his desk, before folding it carefully and placing it in a drawer.

It was a reminder of where unbridled ambition could lead and of the real human cost of corruption's endless cycle.

***

The room held the quiet intensity of a sanctuary—a place where stories of struggle and resilience had been whispered for decades.

Luigi poured two glasses of Sicilian red, the wine catching the last rays of sunlight, transforming into liquid crimson.

Lorenzo sat across from him, his posture revealing tension and anticipation.

The leather chairs, worn smooth by years of confessions and consultations, seemed to hold their own memories.

Instead of answering Lorenzo's unspoken questions about the investigation, Luigi stroked his thick beard—salt and pepper hair catching the light, his eyes distant and reflective.

'You remind me of myself at your age,' Luigi said, his voice carrying the weight of hard-earned wisdom.

'So certain you can change everything through sheer force of will.'

Lorenzo accepted the wine, the glass cool against his fingers.

'What changed?'

The unanswered question felt heavy with meaning.

Settling into his chair, the lawyer's seat groaned, much like an old storyteller about to share a secret.

'I was ten when they killed my father.'

His words fell with surgical precision.

'He was a judge in Palermo, prosecuting a major mafia case. They used a car bomb—very dramatic, very final.'

Lorenzo's hand froze midway to his glass, the weight of Luigi's revelation pressing against the room's careful stillness.

'Few do,' Luigi continued, his Sicilian accent growing stronger, transforming with memory.

'That explosion didn't just end a life. It reshaped an entire world —my world.'

Luigi's narrative unfolded like a carefully preserved manuscript, each word carrying the weight of personal history.

'I threw myself into law school, dreaming of bringing down the entire mafia network,' he said, his fingers tracing the wine glass's delicate rim.

A sad laugh escaped him, a sound that held more complexity than simple amusement.

'Young men have such grand dreams, no?'

The office seemed to contract around them—bookshelves lined

with legal volumes, photographs of family and forgotten cases creating a mosaic of human struggle. Dust motes danced in the last remnants of evening light, silent witnesses to Luigi's confession.

'What happened?' Lorenzo asked, his voice barely above a whisper.

'Reality happened.'

Luigi's response came with the finality of a courthouse gavel.

'In Palermo, the mafia's tentacles reach everywhere—politicians, institutions, the very fabric of society.'

He leaned forward, the leather of his chair sighing beneath his movement, his eyes burning with a fire that decades could not extinguish.

His Sicilian accent thickened, becoming a living testament to his roots, to the history carved into his very speech.

'I watched criminals walk free while good men died. Every victory I won turned hollow—like wine left too long in the sun, losing its promise, its potential.'

The room seemed to breathe with Luigi's memories, the walls absorbing the raw emotion of his narrative.

Lorenzo sat transfixed, the untouched wine before him a forgotten offering to this unexpected confession.

'So you gave up?' Lorenzo's question hung in the air, a delicate challenge wrapped in genuine curiosity.

'No.'

Luigi's response came swift and sharp, his eyes flashing with a intensity that belied his years. The word carried more weight than a simple denial—it was a declaration, a manifesto of survival.

He gestured around his modest surroundings—the cluttered office with its worn wooden shelves, faded photographs, and stacks of case files that seemed to tell their own silent stories.

'Twenty years ago, I moved to Rome and started over. Instead of tilting at windmills, I began helping people I could save—immigrants facing deportation, the wrongly accused, the vulnerable.'

The light shifted, casting longer shadows across the room.

Luigi's hands moved as he spoke, tracing invisible maps of human struggle, of small but significant battles fought in quiet offices like this one.

'Not exactly the career I dreamed of,' he continued, a self-deprecating smile playing at the corners of his mouth.

'I could make ten times more in corporate law. But every time I reunite a mother with her children or save someone from unjust prosecution, I feel my father's spirit.'

Lorenzo studied his wine, the deep red liquid swirling like the complex emotions churning within him.

The office seemed to hold its breath, waiting for the next revelation.

'But doesn't it feel like surrendering?'

The question escaped him, raw and vulnerable—a glimpse into his own internal struggle.

'Ah, there's the question.'

Luigi's smile carried the weight of decades, a landscape of wisdom etched into every line.

He leaned back, with the movement of a man who had witnessed humanity's brightest and darkest moments.

'Let me tell you something about justice, my friend,' he said, his voice dropping to a tone reserved for profound truths.

'It's not always about grand gestures or exposing everything. Sometimes it's about protecting what we can, helping who we can, while staying alive to fight another day.'

His hand reached for the wine bottle—a practised movement that spoke of countless similar conversations, of wisdom shared over glasses of Sicilian red.

'My wife Carla taught me that,' Luigi continued, and something softened in his eyes—a tenderness that suggested love was perhaps the most profound form of rebellion.

'Our children are in America now, living their own lives. We have a small apartment, good friends, excellent wine. It's not the life I imagined when I was filled with revenge, but it's a life with meaning.'

'And you're satisfied with that?' Lorenzo's question carried a hint of challenge, a younger man's scepticism testing the boundaries of compromise.

Luigi's fingers traced the wine glass, a contemplative gesture that suggested depth beyond simple contentment.

'Satisfied?'

The word hung in the air, weighted with nuance.

He stroked his beard thoughtfully, each silvered hair a testament to hard-won wisdom.

'I've learned to find joy in small victories. The system that killed my father is still there, but I've found ways to fight it that don't require martyrdom.'

The office seemed to contract, the space between them charged with unspoken understanding.

Photographs of past cases watched silently from the walls—each frame a reminder of battles fought, of lives touched.

Luigi fixed Lorenzo with a penetrating stare, the kind of look that could cut through pretence and reach the core of a man's soul.

'Which brings us to your crusade.'

Lorenzo shifted uncomfortably, the leather chair groaning beneath his movement a sound that seemed to echo his internal conflict.

'I can't just walk away,' he said, the words a mixture of defiance and uncertainty.

'No one's asking you to.'

Luigi's response was immediate, soft yet unyielding.

'But consider this—maybe there are ways to fight corruption that don't end with you in a suitcase like Marina.'

His voice softened, becoming something between a warning and a prayer.

'Think of what you can lose. Some people need you alive more than the world needs another dead hero.'

Silence filled the office in Piazza Vittorio, heavy as ancient Roman stone.

The last light of day pressed against the dusty windows, painting the room in shades of deepening amber and shadow.

Outside, Rome continued its eternal dance—scooters weaving through narrow streets, distant conversations rising and falling like a urban symphony.

Lorenzo's fingers traced the rim of his wine glass, an unconscious gesture of contemplation.

The weight of Luigi's words settled around him like a cloak, complex and unexpectedly comforting.

'How do you do it?'

His voice broke the silence, raw and vulnerable.

'How do you accept that you can't fix everything?'

Luigi's laugh was unexpected—not bitter, not triumphant, but something in-between.

A sound of hard-earned understanding.

'Who says I've accepted it?'

The corner of his mouth lifted in a smile that spoke volumes.

He reached for the wine bottle.

'The fire that burned in me when they killed my father—it still burns. I've just learned to use it to warm people rather than burn everything down.'

The metaphor hung between them—a bridge between generations, between rage and wisdom, between destruction and hope.

Outside, Rome's streetlights began to flicker to life, casting their own quiet resistance against the gathering darkness.

CHAPTER 6

Lorenzo's phone buzzed as he settled into his usual corner at Gino's, the familiar leather booth creaking beneath his weight.

The restaurant pulsed with a muted energy—a few late-night diners scattered like disconnected constellations, their conversations a low, indistinct murmur.

The scent of rosemary and garlic drifting from the kitchen should have been comforting, but instead, it carried the sharp edge of memory.

Each wisp of aroma transported him back to a night not long ago—Camila seated across from him, her laughter filling the space between them like sunlight, now just a fading photograph in his mind.

His screen blurred as he hesitated, fingers hovering over the send button.

Days of unanswered messages—cold, lingering in read receipts—had conditioned him to expect silence.

Yet a fragile thread of hope still connected him to possibility.

I understand why you needed space. I lost myself in this investigation, and you deserved better. I promise to resolve this soon, to become the man you and Miguel deserve.

The words hung suspended for a breathless moment before he hit send, as if releasing a weight heavier than mere pixels and digital signals.

The screen's dull glow cast shadows across his face—a cartography of uncertainty and hope.

No instant reply came. No acknowledgment.

He pocketed the phone, resolve hardening like cooling metal.

The waiter arrived with gently steaming pasta, a commonplace practice that seemed almost defiant against the complexity of his current existence.

Giovanni's email arrived with the precision of a surgeon's scalpel:

Dear Lorenzo,

The notebook's code was simpler than expected—a basic substitution cypher favoured by certain Camorra factions. The contents are chilling: detailed records of debts and explicit threats of violence against defaulters.

I've identified several victims and plan to warn them discreetly. More concerning—I found your email credentials exposed on dark web forums. Enable two-factor authentication immediately and use a VPN going forward.

Be careful. These people don't play games.

Giovanni

The fork trembled slightly in Lorenzo's hand.

Appetite vanished, replaced by a cold understanding of the stakes.

***

The next morning, Lorenzo walked into Police Headquarters—a building that seemed to breathe institutional memory, its walls holding decades of unspoken stories.

Inspector Albanese's office was minimalistic, a landscape of bureaucratic efficiency. Case files stacked on metal shelves like archaeological layers, the air thick with the scent of burnt coffee and unresolved tensions. Fluorescent lights cast a clinical glare across the cramped space.

'*Dottor* Moretti,' Albanese said, barely glancing up from a desk buried under half-signed documents.

His voice carried the weight of countless investigations.

'I understand you have information about the Marina Ricci case?'

Lorenzo adjusted his tie—a small, deliberate gesture of composure. He sensed the inspector's scrutiny before uttering a single word.

'I have reason to believe Marina Ricci's disappearance isn't what it seems,' he began carefully.

Each word measured, calculated.

'Her financial records suggest she wasn't just hiding funds—she was moving money for someone powerful.'

Albanese sighed, rubbing his temple—a gesture that spoke of exhaustion deeper than mere physical fatigue.

'If you have something concrete, now's the time to share it. Otherwise, you might want to reconsider how deep you're digging.'

It wasn't a threat. It was a warning—the kind whispered between professionals who understood the delicate dance between justice and survival.

***

Days later, Lorenzo stepped into the bank lobby, sensing the shift in atmosphere before anyone spoke.

Conversations quieted like a sudden drop in air pressure. Some colleagues offered stiff, performative nods, while others averted their eyes—each reaction a subtle testament to the scandal that had brushed against his reputation.

Some had expected him to leave. Others had wanted him to.

He wouldn't give them the satisfaction.

From his new office, he watched the familiar flow of clients and employees moving below—a choreography of institutional life that continued regardless of individual dramas.

His return had been negotiated on his terms—no forced resignation, no exile. But the past weeks had left their mark, invisible yet unmistakable.

Lorenzo's gaze swept the lobby, a habit acquired during weeks of investigation.

He scanned the faces in the crowd, each one a blur of anonymity, searching for any sign of someone who didn't belong. A reflex born from weeks of navigating uncertain terrain.

But security, he had learned, was never a contract. It was a fragile illusion.

***

'Three more loan applications from the Ecuadorian community,' Paolo said, dropping the files on the desk with a soft rustle.

'Rosa's friends?'

The question hung between them, weighted with unspoken understanding.

Lorenzo smiled, thinking of the complex network Rosa had woven—part housekeeper, part unofficial community liaison.

'Two of them. She's becoming quite the unofficial loan officer.'

Yet new challenges emerged daily.

Even with his promotion, the immigrant community's expectations sometimes exceeded what he could deliver.

And though Camila stayed over occasionally now, they hadn't discussed living together again. Some wounds needed more time to heal.

But as Lorenzo reviewed the loan applications, a sense of peace settled over him.

***

'Please, Lorenzo,' Rosa pleaded, standing in his office doorway, her posture a mixture of professional deference and personal passion. 'José's family has been in Italy for fifteen years. His repair shop could succeed with just a small loan.'

'Rosa...' Lorenzo rubbed his temples, the gesture betraying his internal conflict.

'You know I can't bypass procedures.'

'This is why people go to Bianchi!' Rosa's voice cracked with frustration, a fissure revealing deeper systemic problems.

'The system forces them to!'

Her words struck Lorenzo like a physical blow, exposing the institutional barriers that transformed survival into a desperate negotiation.

After Rosa left, Lorenzo sat staring at his computer screen, rows of loan rejections blurring into a landscape of bureaucratic indifference.

Hardworking immigrants with solid business plans, reduced to statistical risks by algorithms that knew nothing of human potential.

'There has to be a better way,' he muttered, the words a quiet rebellion against a system that seemed designed to exclude.

***

Paolo found Lorenzo still at his desk in the late hours, surrounded by research papers that transformed the sterile office into a war room of potential change.

'Planning a career change?' he asked, his tone a mixture of scepticism and curiosity.

'Look at this.'

Lorenzo pushed a document across his desk, his finger tracing lines of data that held the promise of alternative thinking.

'The Grameen Bank in Bangladesh. They've revolutionised lending to the poor through micro-loans and peer accountability.'

'Interesting.'

Paolo settled into a chair, the leather sighing beneath him.

'But we're not in Bangladesh.'

'No, but the principle is sound.'

Lorenzo's eyes burned with the intensity of someone who had seen beyond conventional boundaries.

'What if we created something similar here? Legal lending for marginalised communities, without the exploitation.'

Paolo scanned the document, his professional scepticism gradually giving way to genuine interest.

'They've kept default rates impressively low—what, 2 to 8%? That's unheard of, especially in places with such high poverty levels.'

'Exactly,' Lorenzo said, leaning forward.

The overhead light cast sharp shadows across his face, transforming his profile into something between an investigator and a revolutionary.

'Compare that to what we're seeing here. In Italian banks, even with all the bureaucracy, the default rate on loans is still over 4%. If a system like Grameen's can work in Bangladesh, why not adapt it to our conditions?'

'You're talking about introducing micro-loans here?' Paolo asked, his tone a blend of challenge and genuine curiosity.

'Yes, but adjusted for our realities. Grameen uses peer accountability. We could explore legal frameworks that provide affordable, small-scale lending, especially for people who can't access traditional credit. We'd cut out the loan sharks and maybe even drive down non-performing loan rates.'

Paolo leaned back, the chair creaking under the weight of contemplation.

'It's ambitious. But if Grameen can achieve this in one of the most economically challenging environments, maybe there's something we can learn.'

'Exactly,' Lorenzo said. 'We won't copy them outright, but we'd be fools not to adapt their principles.'

***

Lorenzo's apartment became a war room of possibility. Research on micro-lending spread across his coffee table like battle plans, his laptop open with a resignation letter draft—a declaration of intellectual rebellion.

His phone buzzed.

'I've never seen you so determined,' Luigi's voice broke the silence around Lorenzo. You're actually going to do this?'

'I have to try,' Lorenzo said, his voice steady.

'After everything we've seen—the exploitation, the desperation—I can't just watch it continue.'

A long pause stretched between them, pregnant with unspoken understanding.

'I'm proud of you,' Luigi said finally. 'After all, you found a way to use that fire to warm up and not to burn everything down. Cheers to that.'

***

Two months later, Lorenzo convened a secret meeting with his most trusted colleagues.

His colleagues showed a blend of excitement and worry as he explained his vision for the micro-lending initiative. It was a game-changing idea, in direct opposition to everything known about traditional banking and risk assessment.

Lorenzo understood that escaping the ingrained exploitation and corruption in their community required thinking differently to achieve meaningful change.

He spoke with passion about the transformative potential of their work, particularly in improving lives through accessible credit and financial literacy programs. And as he watched his team slowly come around, their scepticism giving way to cautious optimism, Lorenzo felt a glimmer of hope for the first time in months.

A sense of potential filled the room—Paolo, Lucia, and Marco leaning in, their expressions a complex mixture of curiosity and apprehension.

'No collateral requirements,' Lorenzo explained, his voice steady but impassioned.

Sunlight caught the edge of documents spread before them, casting sharp shadows across carefully drawn plans.

'No excessive interest rates. Just character-based lending with peer group accountability. The funding will come from a pool of social impact investors and grants.'

Lucia's eyes widened, reflecting a blend of professional scepticism and genuine excitement.

'It's brilliant,' she said, her tone a delicate balance between awe and hesitation. 'But the regulatory hurdles alone—'

'I've already spoken to lawyers,' Lorenzo interrupted, his resolve cutting through potential objections. 'It's complex, yes, but doable.'

His gaze swept across the room, a silent challenge and invitation.

'I've left the bank to make this happen. I need to know—are you with me?'

Marco, a compliance managing director hesitated, the weight of institutional caution pressing down. Finally, he shook his head regretfully.

'I can't risk my pension, Lorenzo. I'm sorry.'

But Paolo and Lucia exchanged a glance—a silent language of shared conviction.

'We're in,' they said in unison, their words a declaration of belief.

Many months later, *Dottor* Lorenzo Moretti, CFO, stood in the modest storefront housing IAMA, International Association Micro-credit Agency, situated in the heart of Piazza Vittorio.

Sunlight filtered through large windows, casting a hopeful glow across the space that represented more than just a business—it was a promise.

***

Ade's hands trembled slightly as he signed the loan papers, each stroke a testament to newfound possibility.

The Nigerian vegetable vendor's eyes glistened with a mixture of hope and disbelief.

'This will change everything for my family,' he said. 'No one else would give me a chance.'

Lorenzo smiled, remembering Rosa's words about Bianchi. They'd found a better way, after all.

But across town, a different narrative was taking shape.

A Phoenix Corp enforcer read the newspaper article about the new agency, rage building with each paragraph.

His predatory lending territory was being threatened—and that needed addressing.

***

Lorenzo's phone lit up with an unknown number, the screen casting a cold blue light against his skin.

'Ah, the prestigious banker turned saviour of immigrants.'

The voice dripped with contempt, digitally distorted yet unmistakably menacing.

'How noble.'

'Who is this?' Lorenzo demanded, his voice steady despite the unease crawling beneath his skin.

'Call me Enzo. I have a business proposition for you.'

Lorenzo's grip on the phone tightened.

'I'm not interested.'

'Oh, but you will be. You're stealing my clients, you see. Help me out, and we can both profit.'

'Go to hell.'

Enzo's laugh was a razor's edge—cold, sharp, cutting through the routine of Lorenzo's day.

'Careful. It would be a shame if people learned about your questionable practices.'

'You only deal in lies,' Lorenzo replied, ending the call with trembling hands that betrayed the calm surface of his composure.

But Enzo was just getting started.

***

Over the following weeks, rumours spread through the immigrant community like a subtle poison—whispers of fraud, kickbacks, suggestions that IAMA was exploiting the vulnerable through his agency.

Lorenzo and his team fought back with surgical precision.

Transparency became their shield, client testimonials their weapon.

Slowly, truth began to drown out the malicious rumours.

Then came the day that shattered everything.

***

Despite their careful protocols—never going with strangers, always checking with Mama first—kidnappers cornered Miguel and his teacher, using official-looking diplomatic credentials to force their cooperation.

Miguel was gone.

***

Lorenzo held Camila as she crumpled, her screams muffled against his chest—a primal sound of pure maternal anguish that seemed to tear through the very fabric of reality.

Inspector Albanese arrived, his weathered face a mask of professional grimness.

'Professional job,' he said, his words clinical against the raw emotional landscape.

'We're analysing security footage now.'

***

That night, Lorenzo's phone buzzed with a message that would redefine their existence.

The voice on the other end was digitally distorted, but Lorenzo recognised the underlying menace instantly.

'Ponte Mammolo shopping mall. Parking garage. Level B3. One hour. Come alone, or the boy dies.'

***

The garage stretched before him like a concrete tomb, shadows pooling between concrete pillars.

A black Nissan slid into view, its engine a quiet, menacing purr.

Enzo stepped out, his shark-like smile amplified by an expensive suit that seemed to mock the desperation of the moment.

'Where's Miguel?' Lorenzo's voice cracked, a sound more wounded than human.

Enzo snapped his fingers.

Two men emerged from the car, dragging a small, frightened figure between them.

Miguel's eyes were red from crying, fear etched into every line of his young face.

'Papa Lorenzo!' the boy cried out, his voice muffled as one of the men clamped a hand over his mouth.

'Please,' Lorenzo fell to his knees, the concrete cold and unforgiving against his skin.

'He's just a child.'

'Children,' Enzo said coolly, each word a calculated weapon, 'are excellent motivation.'

He tossed a thick envelope at Lorenzo's feet—a damning package containing instructions that would transform everything.

Inside were detailed directions for moving funds through the agency, each page a potential betrayal of everything Lorenzo had built.

'I… I can't…' Lorenzo's words dissolved into a raw, desperate whisper.

Enzo gestured to his men, who began dragging Miguel back toward the car, the boy's small frame seeming impossibly fragile against their brutal movements.

'Wait!' Lorenzo's cry echoed through the parking garage.

He grabbed the envelope with shaking hands, the weight of compromise pressing against his soul.

'I'll do it. Just please, don't hurt him.'

'Wise choice.'

Enzo's smile was reptilian, devoid of human warmth.

'Remember—one wrong move, and the boy disappears forever.'

The Nissan melted into the darkness, taking Miguel with it.

Lorenzo remained on his knees, the envelope a symbol of his capitulation, trembling hands a testament to a father's ultimate vulnerability.

**

At home, Camila's face crumpled when she saw him, transformation happening in an instant from hope to devastation.

'What happened? Where's my son?' she demanded, her voice a razor's edge of maternal terror.

Lorenzo handed her the documents—an elaborate money-laundering scheme that was a physical manifestation of their nightmare.

'He wants me to help him move dirty money through the agency. If I refuse…'

He paused, swallowing hard.

'Miguel was well. Scared, but well.'

Camila's legs gave way, and Lorenzo caught her as they sank to the floor in a tangle of limbs and despair.

The apartment, usually a sanctuary, now seemed a prison of impossible choices.

'What are we going to do?' she sobbed, her voice raw with a pain that seemed to transcend language.

He held her close, his mind racing through scenarios, each more desperate than the last.

He had built the agency to fight predators like Enzo.

But what good were principles if they cost an innocent child his life?

In the suffocating darkness of their apartment, they clung to each other, their prayers for their son and their souls breaking the silence.

'Surely there's another way,' Camila whispered, her voice trembling.

But deep down, they both knew there wasn't.

That was the moment Lorenzo broke.

At dawn, he called Inspector Albanese.

**

'This could work in our favour,' Albanese said thoughtfully.

'With proper surveillance, we could use this contact to bring down Bianchi's entire network.'

'I understand,' Lorenzo said. 'But please—help us make this right.'

***

The warehouse wasn't just a physical location—it was a psychological battleground where power dynamics shifted like tectonic plates.

Lorenzo realised the confrontation was no longer about victory but about navigating the complex machinery of institutional corruption.

Enzo's shark-like grin was a weapon, honed through years of manipulation.

'You think you understand how this works?' he said, his words slicing through the tense air.

'This isn't about money. It's about control.'

Lorenzo met his gaze without flinching.

'Control is an illusion. Systems break. People change.'

The silence between them stretched, heavy and taut—a chess match where the board itself seemed to shift with every move.

Lorenzo leaned into the role Enzo had cast for him, asking carefully rehearsed questions about shell companies and transfer protocols.

'See?' Enzo purred. 'Cooperation isn't so hard.'

At that moment, Lorenzo uttered the prearranged signal phrase: 'Just tell me where to sign.'

The warehouse doors exploded inward.

'Police! On the ground!'

The shouts were deafening, a cacophony of drawn weapons and commands.

Lorenzo spotted Miguel being led out of a side office amidst the chaos.

Ignoring the frenzy, he ran to *his* son and scooped him into his arms.

'Papa Lorenzo,' Miguel sobbed, clutching his father tightly.

'I'm here, *campeón*. You're safe now.'

***

Miguel sat quietly on Lorenzo's couch, small fingers tracing patterns on the leather.

'They spoke Spanish,' he said suddenly, 'but not like Mama or *Abuelo*. Different Spanish.'

Lorenzo knelt beside him. 'What do you mean?'

'Harder…' Miguel's eyes met his, carrying wisdom beyond his years. 'They smiled, but their eyes were scary. Like piranhas on television.'

The boy's observation sent chills down Lorenzo's spine.

Even children could sense the predators circling their lives.

***

Three weeks later, Camila stood at Lorenzo's balcony, her wine untouched.

Her expression was distant. Guarded.

Lorenzo reached for her hand, but she pulled back a fraction—just enough for him to notice.

'Tell me what's wrong,' he said.

She exhaled. 'It's not you, Lorenzo. It's just… I have to think about Miguel. About the life I've built here.'

His fingers tightened around his glass.

'You don't have to run, Camila.'

Her lips parted, but no words came.

A long silence stretched between them before she spoke.

'I spent years ensuring Miguel had stability. Now, suddenly, I'm making choices without thinking about the consequences.'

He searched her face.

'And I'm one of those choices?'

She let out a soft, conflicted laugh.

'You're the one I wasn't prepared for.'

She touched his cheek lightly, lingering for just a second before turning away.

Lorenzo stared at her silhouette, knowing something was shifting between them.

Fear coiled in his gut as he watched Camila's silhouette against the darkening sky.

He'd spent so long building walls around his heart, convinced that his carefully ordered life was enough. Now, facing the possibility of losing her and this unforeseen chance at genuine love, Lorenzo acknowledged his reliance on her, on her unique way of making him feel acknowledged and understood.

The prospect of resuming his old life—empty routines and cold, lonely nights—filled him with unshakeable dread.

***

Lorenzo immersed himself in work, yet his enthusiasm was absent.

Paolo and Lucia gradually took over more responsibilities as Lorenzo spent his days researching Ecuador—neighbourhoods, schools, job prospects.

***

'You're leaving, aren't you?' Paolo asked one morning, finding Lorenzo's office partially packed.

'I have to try, Paolo. I can't just let them go.'

'The organisation needs you.'

'No.' Lorenzo smiled sadly. 'It needs people who are fully present. You and Lucia have proven that.'

He had booked an open-ended ticket to Quito.

His apartment lease was ending, and most of his belongings were in storage.

Some would call it desperate; others, foolish. But Lorenzo knew he couldn't live with the uncertainty, the maybes, the what-ifs.

'You realise she might not want you there?' Lucia asked gently.

'Then I'll know I tried.'

Lorenzo handed her a folder.

'Everything you need to run things is in here. The board approved your promotion yesterday. Congratulations, CFO.'

***

The night before his flight, Lorenzo stood at his window, watching Rome's lights twinkle.

The city had given him purpose, success, and love—and had nearly taken everything away.

Now, he was betting it all on a chance at redemption.

A notification pinged on his phone—a text from Camila: *Miguel asked about you today*.

Lorenzo's hands shook as he typed his reply: *I miss him. Miss you both.*

Three dots appeared, disappeared, then reappeared. Finally, her message came: *Be careful in Quito. The altitude takes getting used to.*

It wasn't forgiveness. It wasn't an invitation. But it was an acknowledgment, and that was sufficient at the time. Tomorrow, he would board a plane carrying nothing but hope and the determination to prove he could be the man they deserved.

Lorenzo looked around his empty apartment one last time, he knew he was finally choosing what truly mattered.

That same night, as he continued packing, Rosa arrived with food he hadn't asked for but desperately needed.

She watched him sort through the remnants of his careful, solitary life.

'You know,' she said, 'when I first started working for you, I thought you were like one of your Caravaggio paintings—all darkness with a hint of light. But now...'

She smiled.

'Now you're stepping into the light yourself.'

'Even if I don't find them?' he asked softly.

'You'll find them.'

Her eyes held a warmth that steadied him.

'Love has a way of lighting the darkest paths. And, Lorenzo, thank you for keeping me on payroll.'

***

Later, alone, Lorenzo stared at the last photo he had of Camila and Miguel.

Whatever had driven them to run, he would help them face it.

He had to believe that.

CHAPTER 7

The engines rumbled beneath him, steady and constant, yet his thoughts were restless.

Lorenzo gripped the armrest, his knuckles whitening.

A decade of life measured in meetings and deadlines had left him ill-prepared for this leap into uncertainty.

The familiar weight of his old Nokia phone pressed against his chest in its breast pocket—one last anchor to routine.

He wondered why he kept it.

Through the window, Rome disappeared beneath cotton-wool clouds, taking with it the comfort of known streets and predictable days.

He traced digits along the rim of his passport, its pages filled with past business trips—each one plotted, scheduled, contained.

Nothing like this journey into the unknown.

***

Madrid arrived in a sterile limbo of fluorescent lights and hurried connections.

In a terminal café, the bitter dregs of an undrinkable espresso grew cold before him; the air smelled faintly of stale coffee and disinfectant.

His phone lay face-down on the plastic table, its silence speaking volumes.

No messages. No missed calls. Just the hollow echo of unanswered questions.

***

The final leg stretched endlessly across the Atlantic. The meal tray before him remained untouched, his appetite lost somewhere between duty and desire.

Outside, clouds shifted like thoughts he couldn't quite grasp.

Was he truly searching for Camila and Miguel, or was he seeking something in himself?

As they descended into Quito, jagged mountain peaks replaced the familiar rolling landscapes of Italy.

The altitude hit him like a physical force as he stepped onto the tarmac, the thin air tightening around his lungs.

Each breath came with deliberate effort, a reminder of how far he'd ventured from his comfort zone.

***

The drive into the city unfolded like a moving fresco of past and present.

Their taxi wove through narrow streets lined with weathered adobe houses, their ochre and deep blue façades reminiscent of a painting he'd once admired in Rome.

The scent of grilled *maíz* and rich coffee drifted through the open window, mingling with the crisp mountain air.

Vendors' voices overlapped in rapid Spanish, their melodic negotiations forming the heartbeat of the city.

***

That evening, Lorenzo wandered into the Old Town, letting the steep cobblestone streets guide him past colonial facades glowing amber in the setting sun.

In a small restaurant, barely larger than his hotel room, he ordered *locro de papa*—a creamy potato soup that warmed him against the mountain chill.

'First time in Ecuador?'

The waiter paused at his table, studying him with the shrewd assessment of someone who had served countless foreigners.

'Is it that obvious?' Lorenzo managed a faint smile, his fingers curled around the earthenware bowl.

The man chuckled, his lined face softening.

'You have that lost look. But not just tourist-lost. You're searching for something, no?'

Lorenzo's smile turned wry.

The man's perception hit closer than he knew.

A mix of English and halting Spanish spilled from him as he shared a condensed version of his story, his voice thick with emotion.

Something about the quiet restaurant, the comfort of the soup, and the waiter's gentle manner broke through his usual reserve.

'Ah... *amor*,' the waiter said knowingly, nodding with a sage expression. 'The best reason to cross oceans.'

***

In the days that followed, Lorenzo established a methodical routine born from years of financial investigation.

Mornings were spent visiting military compounds, showing Camila's photo to increasingly sympathetic but unhelpful officials.

Their eyes would linger on the image, something unspoken passing across their faces before they shook their heads.

Afternoons he dedicated to walking the city, immersing himself in its rhythms while scanning crowds for familiar faces.

He learned to read the subtle shifts in atmosphere between neighbourhoods, noting where a woman and child might be secure, where they might go unnoticed.

Back at the hotel each evening, Isabela, the receptionist, had become his unofficial confidante.

Her desk faced the entrance, giving her a perfect view of everyone who came and went.

'No luck today, *señor?*' she'd ask, her motherly concern plain in her voice.

Each time he shook his head, her expression grew more determined, as though his quest had become her own.

***

One evening, bone-weary from another fruitless day, Lorenzo climbed to the Virgen de Quito statue atop El Panecillo hill.

Below him, the city spread out like a glittering carpet of lights.

The Andes loomed in the distance, dark and unyielding, as if guarding their secrets.

He received a message—a message from Paolo: *How's the search going?*

Lorenzo stared at the screen, unsure how to capture the strange mix of hope and despair that filled his days.

How could he explain that Quito both captivated and frustrated him?

Every day without finding them was a setback, yet the city had embraced him in unexpected ways.

Still looking, he finally replied. *I won't stop until I find them.*

***

'Lorenzo! Finally! We've been worried.'

Paolo's voice crackled through his phone later that morning.

'Sorry for being distant.' Lorenzo paced his small room, the city lights casting shadows across the floor.

'Ecuador has a way of making you lose track of time.'

'And have you found what you're looking for?'

Lorenzo ignored the question.

'Tell me—what's happening in Rome?'

Paolo cleared his throat.

'The micro-lending programme has exploded. Government agencies want to replicate our model. They're asking for presentations, collaborations—'

'There's more.' Paolo's hesitation was palpable even across

continents.

'Several banks in Quito have expressed interest. They want us to establish a permanent branch there. They've offered funding, support—everything we'd need to expand across South America.'

Lorenzo's heart quickened.

'A branch here? In Ecuador?'

'We think you should lead it.'

***

Later that night, Lorenzo stood on his room's small balcony, the cool night air caressing his face.

Below, the city of Quito vibrated with energy—street vendors arguing prices, music floating through the air, conversations merging into an urban melody.

Unwritten stories and untrodden paths stretched ahead, and for the first time since arriving, a glimmer of hope appeared to him.

***

Days passed, and Lorenzo immersed himself in work, letting Camila's trail grow cold.

Then came another message from Paolo: *Don't forget to call Rosa. She's been trying to reach you—seemed urgent.*

Lorenzo typed back absently: *I'll call her soon. First thing tomorrow.*

But tomorrow never came. Meetings with local banks, endless planning sessions, and new alliances consumed him.

Each evening, as he sifted through sparse leads in Quito's

labyrinthine streets, his phone buzzed with messages from Rome—Paolo with updates, Lucia with transition questions.

And Rosa.

Three missed calls in as many days.

Each night, he thought, 'I should call her back,' but exhaustion always won. Tomorrow.

***

One morning, while reviewing proposals in a café near Plaza Foch, his phone lit up again:

Have you spoken to Rosa yet? She has #A&a=~ about

The garbled message cut off.

Lorenzo's thumb hovered over the screen.

Before he could reply, the café owner arrived with a fresh pot of coffee.

He set the phone aside.

***

That night, back in his hotel room, he finally noticed the growing pile of notifications—all marked urgent.

His finger hovered over the call button, but another message from Paolo interrupted:

Big breakthrough with the ministry. Need your input ASAP.

Work first, he decided. Rosa can wait another day.

***

Troubled dreams disturbed his sleep—Quito's winding streets, a familiar voice always just out of reach.

Only Rosa's desperate cry lingered, dissolving before he could understand.

At dawn, disoriented, he checked his phone: another missed call from Rosa.

Her latest message was garbled nonsense. When he tried calling back, the line was busy.

His new life In Quito had promised a fresh start. But, he realised he had traded one form of blindness for another.

Rosa had always been his lifeline to Camila's world.

How many times had she warned him before? Yet he had ignored her again, lost in his vision of the future.

Even Paolo's messages had taken on an urgency he couldn't ignore: *Have you spoken to Rosa yet? She has news!*

Outside, the city stirred—vendors setting up stalls, traffic threading through narrow streets.

Lorenzo's coffee grew cold in his hands.

Could it be? After all this time?

CHAPTER 8

The mountains of San Andrés weren't just geography—they were witnesses. Guardians of secrets, keepers of stories that transcended individual lives.

The ascent into the Andes made Lorenzo feel a physical pressure from the altitude on his chest.

The view underscored the extensive distances he had conquered both across miles and through inner emotional development.

He realised now that his journey wasn't simply about finding Camila and Miguel; it was about understanding the intricate web of human connection that these mountains seemed to echo with every curve of the road.

San Andrés, a small, remote town nestled high in the Andean range, was worlds away from the bustling cities he was used to.

The region combined its dynamic indigenous culture with breathtaking *páramo* landscapes to create stark beauty.

The hillsides showed fields of quinoa and potatoes in colours of subtle greens and earthy ochres while alpacas grazed without rush along the slopes.

The fresh air transported the earthy aroma of moist soil mixed with wildflowers which created such an intense fragrance it seemed holy.

The car passed through winding dirt roads, flanked by steep ravines on one side and endless views of the cordillera on the other.

Lorenzo caught sight of a group of women in traditional dress—bright shawls draped over their shoulders, their wide-brimmed hats tilted against the mountain breeze—as they carried woven baskets of produce toward the market. Their presence, grounded and timeless, struck him as a living testament to resilience.

His preparation for this trip hadn't just been about logistics. It had been meditative—a ritual of transformation. Each document he reviewed, each contact he approached, felt like a prayer—an offering to understanding, to redemption.

San Andrés was more than a destination. It was a place of convergence, where history, culture, and humanity collided.

The surrounding landscape seemed to breathe with possibility, with the understanding that truth was never linear, never simple. It was alive, shifting, demanding patience, compassion, and radical vulnerability.

***

The village appeared suddenly around a bend—a cluster of red-tiled roofs and whitewashed walls nestled between rolling green hills.

His heart quickened.

Somewhere in this serene hamlet, Camila and Miguel might have been building a new life.

As the car pulled into the town's small plaza, dominated by a whitewashed church with a single weathered bell tower, Lorenzo felt the ache in his chest sharpen.

This wasn't just another step in the journey. It was a reckoning. The mountains had borne witness to centuries of triumph and loss, and now they bore witness to him.

'Some journeys,' he muttered to himself, 'aren't about the destination. They're about becoming.'

***

The three-hour journey from Quito had felt otherworldly. Here, time wasn't dictated by clocks but by the position of the sun.

'You're doing the right thing,' Rosa had assured him over the phone when she revealed the latest location for Miguel and Camila. 'But Lorenzo, be careful. If they're hiding, they must have their reasons.'

'The Andes hold many secrets,' Rosa had said on the phone, her voice softening as she spoke of her homeland. 'In these mountains, entire villages have learned to protect those in need. It started during the colonial times, when indigenous communities sheltered those fleeing Spanish rule. That tradition never died—it just changed with each new generation.'

She had paused, choosing her words carefully.

'A friend shared stories about her grandmother's village when I first visited Italy. In the 1980s political turmoil they devised nonverbal warning systems to alert each other to danger. A certain song hummed while washing clothes, a particular way of arranging market stalls—everything could carry a message for those who knew how to read the signs.'

Lorenzo had leaned forward, intrigued.

'And these villages still exist?'

'Some do,' Rosa had replied, her eyes distant with memory. 'But finding them… that's another matter entirely. They don't reveal themselves to outsiders easily. Trust must be earned.'

**

The hotel receptionist greeted him warmly, the heat from a wood-burning stove filling the small lobby. '*¿Primera vez en San Andrés?*' she asked, catching his accent.

'*Sí*, it's my first time,' Lorenzo replied, his voice steady despite the nervous knot in his stomach. 'I'm… visiting friends.'

**

From his room he could see the village square where evening market vendors prepared their stalls. In another life, this view might have filled him with wonder. Now, every face below drew his scrutiny. Every child's laugh made him turn.

He spent the afternoon walking the cobbled streets, showing their photos with careful casualness.

'*Mi familia,*' he said, the phrase both truth and fiction. 'Have you seen them?'

Kind faces offered only confusion, apologetic smiles, and shakes of the head.

With the sun setting, feelings of tiredness and uncertainty started to emerge.

He lit a candle inside the village church. His dwindling hope mirrored the small flame's struggle against the draught.

Unsure who he was speaking to, he whispered, 'Please. Let them be here.'

As he was leaving, an elderly woman touched his arm. A map of wrinkles covered her face, and her intense gaze spoke of many years.

'You're looking for Camila and Miguel,' she said in Spanish—not as a question, but a statement.

Lorenzo's heart stopped. 'You know them?'

The woman studied him, as though weighing his words against something unseen.

'Why have you come?'

'Because…' Lorenzo's voice cracked. 'Because they're my family. Because I love them. Because I crossed an ocean to find them, and I'd cross a hundred more if I had to.'

The woman's expression softened slightly.

'Come with me.'

Outside, the setting sun bathed the mountains in gold. She led him through narrow streets, past curious onlookers, and children playing. With each step, his pulse quickened.

Could this be it?

A wave of honeysuckle perfume, rich and intoxicating, washed over him as he halted before the little blue door nestled within the aged, whitewashed wall. The Bougainville plant overflowed its container while its pink blooms shone brightly in the diminishing sunlight.

'Are they…?' Lorenzo couldn't bring himself to finish the question.

The woman gave him a sympathetic smile.

'They left two weeks ago.'

Her words hit him like a blow. They had remained here for over sixty days yet an unseen force pushed them to relocate once more.

The darkness swallowed them whole; their movements too quick for his eyes to follow, leaving him grasping at air.

His legs were weak. He steadied himself against the blue door as petals fell softly around him.

'But they were here? They were safe?'

'*Sí.*' Her eyes held a mixture of sympathy and something else—worry.

'Camila and the boy seemed... anxious. Like people who feel shadows at their backs. They left in a hurry. A couple of boxes are still here. Take them with you.'

***

That night, he paced the cheap wooden floorboards of his hotel room until they creaked in protest.

The woman's words echoed in his mind: *shadows at their backs.*

What was Camila running from? The troubles in Rome were over, weren't they?

A wave of guilt and anger surged through him. If only he had contacted Rosa when she first tried to reach him...

He grabbed his phone and dialled her number.

'Lorenzo?' Her voice was thick with sleep. 'It's late there.'

'They were in San Andrés, Rosa. But they left two weeks ago.'

He raked a hand through his hair.

'The woman who knew them—something she said bothered me. She mentioned they seemed afraid.'

A lengthy, heavy silence filled the phone call, punctuated only by Lorenzo's shallow breaths, before she finally said, 'there's something I should have told you earlier'.

His heart sank.

'What is it?'

'A week before Camila left Rome, she came to see me. She was terrified. She said someone had been following her and Miguel.'

'Following them?' His voice rose. 'Why didn't you tell me this?'

'She made me promise not to. She said knowing would put you in danger.' Rosa's voice cracked. 'I thought… I thought once they were safe in Ecuador, it wouldn't matter anymore.'

Lorenzo sank onto the bed, his mind racing. 'Did she say who was following them?'

'No. But Lorenzo, listen to me—she wasn't running from you. She was trying to protect you.'

The night pressed heavily against his window, the distant mountains now only shadows under the stars.

Lorenzo thought back to Camila's final days in Rome. Had he missed the signs? Moments when she looked over her shoulder, startled by a noise?

'There's more,' Rosa continued. 'The day before they left, she was accessing some old files. I'm not sure what she found, but… whatever it was, that's when she decided to leave… I think.'

Camila's father had been a high-ranking military officer in Ecuador. Could it have been something related to him?

'Rosa, do you have any idea where I can find her father?'

'No, *mijo*. If Camilla was right—if looking into this is dangerous—'

'Please.' His voice was barely a whisper. 'I can't protect them unless I know what we're up against.'

Another long pause.

'Give me a few days. But Lorenzo? Be careful. If someone is following them—'

'They might be following me too,' he finished, moving to the window.

He scanned the quiet streets of San Andrés. In the shadows between buildings, anything—or anyone—could be hiding.

'I'll call you when I have something,' Rosa promised.

After hanging up, Lorenzo stood at the window, watching the moon cast long shadows across the cobblestones.

Somewhere out there, Camila and Miguel were running from something far bigger than he had imagined.

The question burned In his mind: What secrets lay buried in her past that could cast such long shadows?

And, more chillingly: How many people might die to keep those secrets hidden?

***

'Cuenca,' Rosa's voice was raspy on the phone.

 'Alejandro lives there now. I have his address. It took me a few days, but I managed to track him down. Carmen helped me.'

Lorenzo's grip tightened on the phone.

'You found him?'

'Yes, but—be careful. Whatever Camila's running from, it might have started with her father,' Rosa said softly, stirring her coffee.

'he carries himself like the military man he is…'

***

The drive to Cuenca carried Lorenzo through valleys carved by the hands of gods, their green depths cradling rivers that glimmered like molten silver in the midday sun.

Towering eucalyptus trees lined the edges of the Pan-American Highway, their scent sharp and cleansing as it drifted through the open car window.

Villages dotted the landscape, where adobe houses with red-tiled roofs stood nestled among fields of maize and sugarcane.

In these quiet hamlets, time seemed to move as slowly as honey, each moment stretched by the steady rhythms of mountain life.

As he approached his destination, the landscape began to shift. The city, with its iconic skyline of domed cathedrals, emerged like a jewel in the Andean highlands. Red rooftops sprawled across the rolling hills, while the Río Tomebamba cut through the city, its waters tumbling over smooth boulders. Balconies adorned with blooming geraniums leaned over the riverbanks, their vibrant colours a striking contrast to the colonial whitewashed walls.

Yet, for all its beauty, the scenery blurred in Lorenzo's mind, eclipsed by the whirlwind of questions that refused to settle.

Untold stories filled the air which blended with the delicate aromas of roasting coffee and fresh bread that rose from the city's numerous cafés.

The vehicle navigated through Cuenca's central area moving along cobblestone roads while vendors at lively markets offered bright textiles and intricate figurines for sale. Lorenzo's eyes drifted toward the grand Catedral Nueva, its striking blue domes rising like a promise against the clear mountain sky.

But even this sense of grandeur failed to soothe the ache in his chest.

Cuenca was a crossroads—a place where history and modernity collided, much like the questions gnawing at Lorenzo's mind. Somewhere amidst these ancient streets and rushing rivers lay the threads he needed to untangle.

***

The house sat back from the street, partially concealed behind the lavender bloom of jacaranda trees.

Lorenzo's knock resounded against the heavy wooden door, the sound almost swallowed by the quiet of the surroundings.

Footsteps approached—measured, deliberate, and unhurried.

The man who opened the door exuded an aura of authority. Perhaps this was what Miguel thought of him when they met at the museum, when hinting at their resemblance.

His posture betrayed years of military discipline, even in retirement, but his eyes held a weight of sadness that tightened something in Lorenzo's chest.

'*¿Qué es lo que quiere?*' Alejandro's voice was rough, gravel tinged with smoke.

'*Señor, mi nombre es Lorenzo Moretti. Estoy buscando a Camila.*'

Something flickered in Alejandro's eyes—recognition? Fear? For a moment, the older man stood motionless before his gaze hardened.

The conversation continued in Spanish.

'Who are you to speak her name?'

'Someone who loves her,' Lorenzo said, his voice steady.

'Someone who crossed an ocean to find her.'

The silence between them was charged, like the pause before a storm. Then, slowly, Alejandro stepped aside.

'Come in. But understand—some questions are better left unanswered.'

The house bore the precise organisation of a military mind—photographs arranged with mathematical precision, books aligned perfectly on their shelves. Yet amid this rigid order, Lorenzo noticed small disruptions: an empty frame face-down on a side table, a chair pulled slightly askew.

The place felt like a shrine to memories. Photographs lined the walls: Camila as a child, cradled in her mother's arms; her graduation day, beaming with pride. There was Miguel as a baby, his chubby face breaking into a toothless grin. But the more recent frames were conspicuously empty, like missing chapters torn from a story.

'Tea or coffee?' Alejandro offered, leading Lorenzo into a sunlit kitchen.

'Thank you, tea would do,' Lorenzo replied, his voice subdued.

Alejandro moved with precision as he prepared the tea, his actions almost mechanical.

'You met her in Rome?'

'Yes,' Lorenzo said, accepting the steaming cup. He lied without thinking. 'At the bank where I worked. She changed my life.'

'She has that effect.' Alejandro's smile was faint, brittle. 'But you don't know everything about her.'

'I know she's running from something,' Lorenzo countered. 'Something that started long before Rome.'

The older man's hands trembled slightly as he set the teapot down. 'My daughter... she carries burdens you can't imagine. Secrets that could—'

He stopped abruptly, his mouth tightening as if sealing the words away.

'Could what?' Lorenzo pressed, leaning forward.

'It doesn't matter.' Alejandro's tone grew sharp, a defence mechanism.

'She chose to disappear. Perhaps it's better this way.'

'Better for whom?' Lorenzo set his untouched cup on the table. 'Someone's following her, sir. She and Miguel aren't just running—they're hiding.'

The colour drained from Alejandro's face.

'Following her? Are you certain?'

'A friend of ours, Rosa, told me. Before they left Rome last August, Camila orchestrated their departure with extreme care to avoid detection.'

Alejandro sank into his chair, his shoulders sagging under an invisible weight. 'Then it's starting again. I thought... I hoped—'

'What's starting again?' Lorenzo demanded. 'Please, I need to understand.'

The old soldier's gaze drifted to the window, where jacaranda petals fluttered like purple snow.

'I discovered something about Camila—a truth that could've consumed her. I tried to warn her, to advise her, but...' His voice cracked. 'Some secrets cast long shadows.'

'Let me help her,' Lorenzo pleaded. 'Tell me what she's running from.'

Alejandro's eyes met his, filled with anguish and indecision.

'I can't,' he said finally. 'But know this—if you find her, if you truly want to protect her, you'll face things that will test everything you believe. Are you ready for that?'

Lorenzo didn't hesitate.

'Yes.'

The silence stretched as Alejandro studied him, his expression unreadable.

Finally, he nodded, almost imperceptibly.

'Then perhaps… perhaps you're worthy of her after all.'

He stood slowly, his movements heavy.

'I don't know where she is. I've had no contact with her. I haven't seen her in years.'

***

The return drive to Quito that night felt longer, the dark valleys and towering mountains closing in around him. Lorenzo barely noticed the beauty of the starlit sky, though the stars seemed to pulse with urgency, mirroring the storm of thoughts in his mind.

Somewhere in Ecuador, Camila and Miguel were hiding from a danger rooted in secrets and the ambitions of powerful men.

And now Lorenzo had a new destination—one that memories alone could not reach.

CHAPTER 9

Lorenzo's hands trembled as he held Camila's letter, the familiar curves of her handwriting pulling him into a storm of emotions. Each word leapt off the page, her voice whispering into his heart. The plea to stop searching for her and Miguel tore at his soul.

Lorenzo, she had written, *I hope this letter finds you well and safe. I cannot begin to express the conflict in my heart as I write these words, but I must implore you to stop your search for us. It is dangerous, not just for you, but for Miguel and me.*

Her words wove a mosaic of love and fear, gratitude and warning. She spoke of forces beyond their control, dangers she couldn't explain, shadows that threatened to consume them all. *I know you have an unyielding determination,* she wrote, *but there are things we cannot understand or fight.*

***

Grief weighed down Lorenzo's steps as he drifted like a ghost through Quito's streets, the passing weeks blurring into months. Camila's presence permeated his surroundings; he saw her in the markets' bright colours, children's laughter in the parks, and the locals' warm smiles.

His world felt empty and devoid of purpose, a stark contrast to the vibrant life he had known with her. Only the faint whisper of wind through unseen branches accompanied the silence, a silence that felt vast and cold, matching the emptiness in his heart.

He threw himself into his work with a desperate fervour, the stale air of the office and the pressure of deadlines a stark contrast to the dull ache in his chest. But even as Lorenzo poured his heart and soul into the foundation, the echoing silence of the Ecuadorian mountains and forests seemed to amplify the emptiness he felt inside.

***

Lorenzo walked through the quiet, cobblestone streets of Quito, the echo of Camila's laughter in Rome still ringing faintly in his ears; the scent of roasted coffee and distant church bells a stark contrast to the memory of Roman trattorias.

The weight of their respective choices pressed down on them —hers, a heavy burden of responsibility, each decision a lead weight in his heart. An unspoken tension, a palpable shift in their dynamic, marked the end of that chapter, though neither had uttered a single word about it.

A nagging feeling that he'd overlooked something vital, something tiny yet significant, pricked at him, then faded like a forgotten dream. The questions piled up before him, a heavy weight of unanswered queries, each one a challenge that seemed insurmountable.

***

Days bled into each other in a monotonous stream, a repetitive cycle of identical tasks and empty moments, leaving no distinct memories.

Lorenzo buried himself in work, pouring every ounce of energy into the new branch in Quito. Yet memories of Camila haunted him at every turn.

His heart felt like a barren landscape, devoid of life and echoing with the silence of her absence; his professional triumphs felt hollow, unable to bridge the chasm.

His colleagues noticed the change. Though his passion for the work remained, a quiet sadness shadowed his every step. The office thrived yet Lorenzo faced sleepless nights filled with questions.

***

While he was getting ready to exit the hotel for his appointment, the receptionist interrupted him to say: '*Señor* Moretti you have a delivery waiting.'

The little package had only his name written in recognisable curves of Camila's handwriting without any return address.

A tremor seized his hands while he peeled apart the brown paper.

A leather-bound journal lay within the package featuring a cover that had softened with time.

Opening it, he found Camila's elegant script on the first page, her words reaching out to him like a whisper across the distance:

Lorenzo,

I hope this journal finds you well. You told me to stop looking for us yet I needed to say goodbye before leaving. Writing words can sometimes feel easier but leaving you was the most difficult experience of my life.

I want to share everything with you but it's impossible. You are an exceptional person who doesn't deserve to live such a perilous existence. The demons from my past were out of my control so I protected you from that darkness.

My feelings for you remain genuine from the past to today. The memories of you shining through my dark times hold immense value to me.

This journal is my way of keeping you close, even if we're worlds apart. Write in it, tesoro. Pour your thoughts and feelings onto these pages. Perhaps this will keep our hearts connected.

Take care of yourself, my love. Keep building the beautiful life you started in Ecuador. I'll always be watching from afar, wishing you happiness and peace.

With all my love,

Camila

Lorenzo clutched the journal to his chest, his eyes closed against the wave of emotions.

Her words, like her presence, were both a comfort and a wound. He knew he would carry her with him always, their connection etched into his very soul, even as their paths diverged.

***

In the weeks that followed, the journal became Lorenzo's confidant. Each evening, he sat by his window overlooking Quito's twinkling lights and poured his heart onto its pages. He wrote about the organisation's progress, the streets he walked that still echoed with memories of her presence, and the dreams that refused to fade despite their impossible nature.

Some entries were simple accounts of his day:

The micro-lending programme approved ten new loans today. I thought of how you would have smiled at the recipients' joy.

Others revealed the depths of his longing:

I saw a little boy in the plaza today who laughed like Miguel. For a moment, my heart forgot how to beat.

Gradually, imperceptibly, the raw edges of his loss began to soften.

Under his guidance, the Ecuadorian branch flourished, giving him a sense of purpose that—though different from the love he had lost—filled his days with meaning.

Yet, late at night, he would reread Camila's letter, searching between the lines for clues about the darkness she feared.

The journal's pages slowly filled with his thoughts, hopes, and unanswered questions.

Though he knew she might never read them, writing to Camila aided him in believing their hearts remained connected across the separating distance.

Despite his determination to stop searching, he couldn't dismiss the intuition that their paths would cross again.

***

A year passed. Rosa occasionally sent updates about Alejandro, still living his quiet life in Cuenca and steadfastly claiming no knowledge of his daughter's whereabouts.

Lorenzo focused on building his future in Ecuador, but the past refused to release its hold on his heart.

Then, nearly thirteen months after leaving Rome, came the email that changed everything.

A message he had been waiting for appeared in his inbox.

The name in the subject line hit him like a blow: *Silvio Bianchi*.

Lorenzo's blood ran cold as he opened the attached newspaper article.

Rome's police had dealt a significant blow to Bianchi's criminal empire, arresting several key members of his organisation.

***

Rosa's network of contacts expanded, each new connection potentially holding the key to finding them.

A local contact mentioned a village deep in the Andes—Quinua, a place where outsiders rarely ventured. Something in the description resonated with Lorenzo, triggering an instinct he couldn't explain.

***

The journey to Quinua tested Lorenzo's resolve.

The mountain roads wound steeply through the Andean highlands, each turn revealing sheer cliffs and plunging valleys. Mist clung to the peaks, and intermittent rain slicked the narrow paths, making the drive treacherous.

Lorenzo gripped the steering wheel tightly, pressing on with a determination he couldn't fully explain, the altitude thinning the air and sharpening his focus.

Quinua emerged from the landscape as if hidden by design. The village on the mountain slope consisted of small stone and adobe constructions with sloping red-tiled roofs arranged like a patchwork. Chimneys emitted smoke which moved slowly through the fresh air while combining with the smell of damp grass and burning wood. Fields of quinoa and maize covered terraces carved into the hillsides with vibrant green and yellow hues standing out against the muted grey sky.

In the village square, Lorenzo found a modest chapel, its whitewashed walls weathered by time. A few villagers gathered near a fountain at the centre, filling clay jugs with water and chatting in Quechua, their voices rising and falling like music against the quiet.

Women in traditional Andean dress, their brightly coloured shawls pinned with silver *tupus*, carried baskets of produce from the surrounding farms, their woven skirts swaying as they walked.

Children chased each other through the square, their laughter echoing off the stone walls, while a llama tethered nearby watched the scene with lazy indifference.

Lorenzo approached his inquiries with care, showing Camila and Miguel's photos with a practised air of casualness.

At first, the villagers responded politely but cautiously, their expressions guarded, their words measured. Some shook their heads and returned to their tasks, while others glanced at the photos a moment too long before offering clipped responses in Spanish. Their eyes, however, betrayed the weight of unspoken truths.

The air felt heavy with the past, as if the village itself carried the burden of centuries.

Lorenzo couldn't shake the feeling that somewhere amidst the guarded words and watchful gazes lay the faintest thread of a clue.

The mountains, ancient and unyielding, seemed to urge him onward, their silent presence both a comfort and a challenge.

***

As dusk settled over the mountains, he found himself beside a rushing stream, its waters singing of patience and persistence.

The sun's last rays painted the mountains gold as Lorenzo considered his next move.

'Perhaps Camila and Miguel are creating a new life here,' he thought.

What would he do when he finally found them?

The stream murmured beside him, offering no answers.

Yet as darkness blanketed Quinua, Lorenzo felt something stir within him—something he hadn't experienced in months: hope.

CHAPTER 10

'Are you lost, stranger?'

The soft voice startled Lorenzo from his thoughts.

Turning, he saw an elderly man watching him, his eyes holding the wisdom of the mountains themselves.

'Not lost,' he replied, introducing himself. 'Searching.'

He gestured to a nearby bench and sat beside him with the unhurried grace of someone accustomed to the weight of secrets.

'In a place like this, secrets are not readily revealed,' he said. 'But the mountains have a way of guiding those in need.'

There was something in his tone that made Lorenzo open up.

He told him everything—the story of Rome, love found and lost, and the mysterious circumstances that had brought him to these heights.

He listened with the stillness of ancient stones, his expression both knowing and guarded.

'Love can be a powerful force,' he said finally. 'It leads people to do extraordinary things, even leaving everything behind.'

He paused, his weathered hands folding in his lap.

'But love can also be dangerous, especially when it is intertwined with the past.'

Lorenzo leaned forward. 'You know something about them, don't you? Please—they might be in danger.'

The man's hand rested on Lorenzo's, his touch both a warning and a comfort.

'The path you seek is treacherous. The darkness that follows them may consume you, too.'

'I don't care,' Lorenzo said fiercely. 'I love them. I won't rest until I know they're safe.'

He studied the foreigner for a long moment, as though weighing his soul.

Finally, he nodded.

'Very well. The mountain whispers speak of a hidden cave above the village. It is said to hold ancient secrets—a refuge for those who need to disappear.'

Hope flickered in Lorenzo's chest.

'They might be there?'

'Perhaps,' he said. 'But remember—the cave guards its secrets fiercely. Only those destined to find it will.'

***

The mountain path tested every ounce of Lorenzo's resolve.

As he climbed, memories of Rome swirled in the thin air—Marina's investigation, the corruption, the threats that had torn his life apart.

Yet something stronger pulled him forward, beyond exhaustion and fear.

At sunset, the cave emerged like a shadowy threshold, its entrance hidden among jagged rocks. As he moved deeper into the shadows, he could smell the earthy fragrance of moss mixed with wet stone.

His heart pounded not because of physical effort but due to the pressure of his expectations.

***

'Camila?' he called, his voice echoing through the cavern. 'Miguel?'

At first, only silence answered. Then, a faint glow flickered deeper within. It was a small cabin at the other end of the cave. It was in a natural amphitheatre created by the mountains' walls.

He entered the cabin, following towards a chamber where candles cast trembling light on old walls.

And there they were.

Camila looked up; her dark eyes wide with disbelief. Miguel rested next to her while his petite body curled up against her side.

'You shouldn't have come,' she whispered so softly her voice was almost silent.

'I had to,' Lorenzo said, his voice steady but raw with emotion. 'You can't ask me to walk away and expect me to obey.'

Camila sighed, her gaze shifting to Miguel. 'You don't understand what you've risked by coming here.'

'Then make me understand,' he urged, kneeling before her. 'I deserve the truth.'

Her eyes lost focus and her lips quivered as she paused before speaking. She pulled her knees close to her body and wrapped her arms around them to protect herself from the burden of her words.

'Lorenzo listen carefully because there is not just one truth to share. There are many, and each one is harder than the last.'

She inhaled shakily.

'But the hardest truth… is about us—about how we really met.'

Lorenzo felt his chest tighten, a sense of dread knotting his stomach. He said nothing, giving her the space to continue.

'The exhibition, our encounter… it wasn't chance.'

Her hands shook as they rested in her lap.

'Bianchi arranged everything. The tickets, Miguel getting lost… even Marina's involvement. Every moment was orchestrated.'

The silence that followed was crushing, as though the air in the room had turned to lead.

Stunned into silence Lorenzo's thoughts whirled as he struggled to make sense of their shared love alongside her calculated manipulation.

Camila spoke in a whisper so faint she needed to repeat herself when she told him, 'there is another thing I need to reveal to you. The notebook you received back in Rome—'

Lorenzo's breath caught. 'You sent it to me?'

'Yes.'

Her eyes met his, filled with a mixture of regret and vulnerability.

'I hoped that if you delivered it to the police, it would give you the closure you needed—that you'd stop searching, for me and for answers.'

A sad smile played at her lips.

'I should have known better. You've never been one to leave a story unfinished.'

'Even when the story was about my own deception?' Lorenzo asked, his voice low and steady, though it carried an undertone of pain.

Camila flinched but didn't look away.

'The bank had become a problem for Bianchi,' she continued. 'Giorgio was becoming reckless—demanding more money, threatening to expose everything if they didn't meet his terms. He was a liability.'

She paused, her voice growing heavier with each word.

'They needed someone to replace him. Someone clean. Respected. Someone whose reputation was beyond reproach.'

Her dark eyes locked onto his.

'That's why they chose you.'

'And you?' Lorenzo asked softly. 'How did they have such power over you?'

Camila took a shaky breath, her gaze dropping to her hands.

'That story begins in Ecuador. My father wasn't just any military officer—he headed intelligence operations investigating corruption within the armed forces. He uncovered a network of officers involved in drug trafficking, taking bribes to allow shipments through military checkpoints. And Jorge… Jorge was one of them.'

Lorenzo's brow furrowed as the weight of her words sank in.

'I didn't know when I married him,' Camila continued, her voice trembling.

'He was charming, ambitious—everything a young woman might want. But then I found documents in his office: shipment routes, payoff schedules… proof of everything. When I confronted him, he confessed it all.'

'What did you do?' Lorenzo asked, his voice gentle but urgent.

'I was young, pregnant with Miguel, and terrified. Jorge convinced me we could start over in Italy. He had connections—Bianchi's organisation. They arranged everything for us: a new identity for Jorge, a position for me at the consulate. But there was a price.'

Her voice cracked.

'The consulate job wasn't just a job. The old consul was part of the organisation. They used me, knowing who my father was, to facilitate document fraud. I helped them move people and money through diplomatic channels and—worst of all—passed them confidential information about my father's investigations. By the time I realised how deep it went, I was trapped. Jorge abandoned us, fleeing back to Ecuador, but Bianchi still owned me.'

Her voice grew quieter.

'My father resigned his post in shame, though he never publicly declared why. But he never forgave me. He never spoke to me again.'

Lorenzo's heart ached for her, but questions still burned within him.

'And why did they choose you to get close to me?'

Camila hesitated, shame flickering across her face.

'Marina tried herself, but you were too reserved, too cautious. You didn't take any notice of her. They even started to think you might be gay. I was their last chance. They thought I was perfect—a single mother, an immigrant like Rosa, someone who could appeal to your protective nature.'

Her voice faltered, trembling with emotion.

'What they didn't count on… was that at the party in Rocca Priora, watching you with my friends, seeing your genuine kindness and warmth… I would fall in love with you. Truly fall in love.'

Lorenzo swallowed hard, his heart twisting at her confession.

'What happened when they realised?'

'At first, Marina thought it was funny,' Camila said, bitterness creeping into her voice. 'She was too caught up in her own schemes to see the danger. You see, she'd started playing both sides—helping Bianchi set up his replacement for Giorgio while building her own operation. That's why she spoke to you about the Trastevere files. She was skimming money, making her own plans. She thought she was untouchable.'

'But something doesn't add up,' Lorenzo interrupted, frowning. 'If I was meant to replace Giorgio, why did Marina try to frame me?'

'Because she wanted everything,' Camila explained, her voice steady but heavy with grief. 'She was secretly trying to take over. By framing you, she thought she could eliminate both you and Giorgio at once, clearing the way for her own ascent. She believed she was clever enough to double-cross Bianchi himself.'

Camila's voice dropped, a shadow passing over her face.

'Her arrogance cost her life.'

Lorenzo stiffened.

'What happened to her?'

Camila's voice tightened, her words coming slowly, as if the memory physically hurt.

'When Bianchi discovered her betrayal, he... he made an example of her. The way they killed her, what they did to her body—it was a message to everyone in the organisation. No one was untouchable.'

Lorenzo's fists clenched, his jaw tightening.

'Did you try to leave?'

'I begged them to let me go,' Camila said, her voice raw with emotion. 'But they knew I'd seen too much. I knew too much. The threats started—subtle at first. Hints about Miguel's safety, reminders of my imposter status. And then... then they took him. Not just to punish me for falling in love with you, but to show me what happens to those who defy them.'

Her tears fell freely now, but she made no move to wipe them away.

'Yet you still chose to run,' Lorenzo said softly, his voice filled with a mixture of admiration and sorrow.

'Because of you,' she whispered, her eyes meeting his. 'Watching you fight for Miguel, risk everything to save him—it gave me courage. And after seeing what they did to Marina, I knew we had to disappear completely. Giorgio never knew about their plans to replace him, or my role in it all. But Bianchi's reach... it was everywhere. I couldn't trust anyone.'

Lorenzo nodded, the pieces of her story finally fitting together.

'So you came back to Ecuador.'

'Because I needed to face my past to protect our future. My father—for all his faults—still has connections in the military. He may not approve of my choices, but he wouldn't let harm come to his grandson.'

She gestured to their surroundings.

'This cave has been a sanctuary for people fleeing violence for generations. The local community protects it and guards its secrets. I was expecting you and, I suppose, Ramiro told you about the cave.'

Lorenzo absorbed everything, seeing their entire relationship in a new light.

The art exhibition, Miguel's wandering, their early conversations—all had been orchestrated. Yet their love had grown despite the manipulation, perhaps even because of it.

'I understand if this changes everything,' Camila whispered. 'If you can't forgive—'

'Stop,' Lorenzo interrupted, taking her hand. 'Yes, it hurts to know our meeting was planned. But you broke free from their control because of love. You chose to protect me, to protect us, even when it meant losing everything.'

He touched her cheek gently.

'Our beginning might have been orchestrated, but our love rewrote the story.'

Miguel stirred in his sleep, mumbling softly. They both looked at him, remembering his joy when Lorenzo had saved him, the pure trust in his eyes.

'They underestimated us,' Lorenzo said quietly. 'They thought they could use love as a weapon, but real love became their undoing.'

Camila leaned into his embrace, her tears soaking his shirt. 'I've been so afraid to tell you. Afraid it would destroy what we have.'

'Nothing could destroy this,' he assured her. 'Not Bianchi, not Marina, not even the truth about our past. What matters is who we chose to become, together.'

The old walls seemed to hold their secrets close, understanding that sometimes the most honest love can grow from deception's soil, transforming manipulation into something pure and true.

Outside, the mountain kept its eternal vigil, guardian of a love that had refused to be denied by fear, distance, or the dark shadows of the past.

He reached out, his hand brushing hers.

'You've been running for so long. Let me help you stand still.'

Her eyes glistened with unshed tears.

'I can't let you risk yourself for us. I won't.'

His voice hardened.

'You don't get to decide that for me. I've already made my choice, Camila. And I'm not leaving without you.'

A weighty silence enveloped the cabin, which the distant sound of dripping water interrupted.

After staring at him intently for several seconds, and hearing about the developments in Rome about Bianchi's organisation, Camila gave her assent as a small ray of hope pierced through her weariness.

Their kiss was gentle and tender, a homecoming rather than a victory.

Miguel's arms wrapped around them both, completing the circle of their makeshift family.

The candles flickered, casting their joined shadows on walls that had sheltered countless secrets through the ages.

Lorenzo shared everything—the letter that had both crushed and sustained him, the endless searching, and the mysterious path that had directed him to this sacred place. She listened intently, her eyes never leaving his face, while her *hijo* slept close beside her, their hands intertwined.

'I thought I was protecting you by staying away,' she said softly, regret threading through her words. 'But I realise now that love isn't about shielding each other from the world. It's about facing challenges together.'

His fingertips caressed her cheek gently as he said: 'I understand why you left but being apart from you is too much for me to bear.'

Her grip tightened on his hand.

'Silvio Bianchi is more dangerous than you know. He'll stop at nothing to get what he wants. Even in prison.'

'Fear will no longer rule our existence,' Lorenzo said with conviction.

Her eyes held shimmering tears which reflected hope instead of despair.

'You truly are remarkable. I don't know what I did to deserve you.'

'Love isn't earned,' he replied softly. 'It's given freely, without conditions.'

***

Their return to Quito marked the beginning of a new chapter.

Though Bianchi's empire was crumbling, the threat he posed remained real.

Using Lorenzo's contacts and the organisation's resources, they found sanctuary in a remote corner of Ecuador. Their secluded haven fostered a life unimaginable back in Rome.

Together, they decided to transform this dark inheritance into light, establishing a Foundation to help victims of organised crime escape their circumstances, while continuing with the microcredit initiative.

The years that followed were a testament to love's healing power. They filled their home with laughter and their days with purpose.

They returned to Quinua, the cave that had reunited them, every year—a place to remember that love could overcome any obstacle.

When they finally heard about the arrests of Silvio Bianchi and his partners, it felt less like triumph and more like release. Haunting shadows faded, replaced with the comforting reality of their life together.

***

Lorenzo's phone buzzed in the thin mountain air. Inspector Albanese's name lit up the screen.

'Lorenzo,' Albanese's voice crackled through the poor connection.

'In the past months, we've finished decoding Marina's notebook and other documents. For obvious reasons I couldn't contact you, but it's over… there was more to this than we thought.'

Lorenzo pressed the phone closer, moving to find better reception.

'Tell me.'

'Marina was playing a dangerous game. Not just embezzlement and loan fraud—she was orchestrating a complete takeover within the bank. Her notes detail how she was positioning herself to replace Salvini while simultaneously building her own operation.'

'Replace Giorgio?'

'Yes. She had dates, amounts, details of his demands to Bianchi. She was documenting Salvini's instability, creating a paper trail of his mistakes. But here's what's interesting—there are references to another plan, something bigger. She mentions a "perfect replacement" but never names them.'

Lorenzo's hand tightened on the phone, realising she had been documenting the very plot she was part of.

'The pattern was there all along,' Albanese continued. 'She was building leverage against everyone—Giorgio, Giancarlo, even Bianchi himself. She thought she could outmanoeuvre them all.'

'And that's what got her killed,' Lorenzo said softly.

'Exactly. But here's what bothers me—some of these operations required inside help from the consulate. Diplomatic cover for moving money. Marina couldn't have managed that alone.'

Lorenzo's breath caught. 'What are you saying?'

'I'm saying be careful, even in Ecuador. Bianchi's network goes deeper than we thought, and it reaches far beyond Rome. People who knew about those consulate operations are either dead or have disappeared.'

Albanese paused meaningfully.

'Stay alert, Lorenzo. Sometimes the best evidence is hidden in plain sight.'

The call ended, leaving Lorenzo with the haunting realisation that nobody truly understood the extent of the whole plot. Or, perhaps, Albanese understood everything.

***

Lorenzo's laptop glowed in his dimly lit hotel room in Quito during one of his business trips. Giorgio's face filled the screen. Even through the digital interface, the tension was palpable. Behind him, a police officer was standing and looking at the screen.

'You wanted to talk,' Giorgio said, adjusting his tie. 'So talk.'

'Why?' Lorenzo asked simply, the question carrying across continents.

Giorgio's usual composure cracked slightly, the video feed catching his subtle flinch. 'You don't understand what it was like. The pressure, the threats. When Bianchi approached me...'

'You could have come to me, or escalated to your superior. We could have fought this together.'

'Fought?'

His disgraced boss's bitter laugh crackled through the speakers.

'You still don't get it. Bianchi owns half of Rome. The loans, the money-laundering—it was just the tip of the iceberg. I made a choice to survive in a system that crushes anyone who doesn't play by its ruthless rules.'

Lorenzo leaned closer to the screen.

'By sacrificing innocent people? By letting Marina die?'

'Marina was stupid. She thought she could outsmart Bianchi.'

The HD video caught every hardening line in Giorgio's face.

'I gave her every chance to play by the rules. But she wanted more—always more.'

'And me? Why try to frame me?'

'Because you were too clean, too righteous, too… lame. There were some cracks in the system and we needed someone to take the fall, and your reputation made you perfect. You matched what we were looking for: reserved, quiet, discreet, single, and introverted. Who would believe the honourable Lorenzo Moretti could have such stamina to fight back?'

Giorgio's smile was cold, distorted slightly by the video lag.

'Until you met your Ecuadorian girl. We underestimated you. Then you became… unpredictable.'

Lorenzo felt a chill despite the warm Ecuadorian night.

'You really think Bianchi will protect you now?'

'He doesn't have to.' Giorgio reached for something off-screen, then held up an envelope to the camera. 'My testimony bought my freedom. Full immunity.'

'There's no immunity from conscience, Giorgio.'

Lorenzo moved to end the call, but Giorgio's voice stopped him.

'Watch yourself, Moretti. Distance won't protect you. Bianchi never forgets his enemies, even behind bars.'

It was the second time in days he had been warned.

The screen went black. Outside his window, the lights of the capital twinkled innocently, but now every shadow seemed to hold potential threats. He understood with crushing clarity why Camila had chosen such remote hiding places.

***

A few weeks later, Paolo sent Lorenzo a link to a local newspaper's website. As he read the article, he felt relief.

Bank Scandal Unveiled: Embezzlement, Betrayal, and the Fall of a Crime Syndicate.

The article's opening was daunting.

A recent investigation has revealed a shocking conspiracy involving key figures at the renowned banking institution Banca EllePi S.p.A. The scheme, orchestrated by a network of insiders, aimed to embezzle millions and establish a criminal syndicate.

Among the perpetrators was Marina Ricci, who vanished under suspicious circumstances, before her body was found in a suitcase in the Roman countryside. Evidence uncovered by investigators links her to the theft of corporate funds and plans to establish an independent illicit financial operation. However, her untimely demise, now confirmed as a murder at the hands of Silvio Bianchi's organisation, disrupted the network's plans and exposed deeper corruption.

Key revelations suggest that Giorgio Salvini, a senior manager at Banca EllePi, played a dual role. While he initially collaborated with Ricci and her associates, Salvini later betrayed them, offering crucial evidence to Bianchi in exchange for immunity. His testimony with the investigators in Rome revealed the syndicate's plans and international connections to larger criminal enterprises. Because of inconsistencies in his story, the authorities revoked Salvini's plea deal, and he now faces charges alongside the other criminals.

Reports surfaced here and there, detailing other information.

The investigation identified Lucio Giancarlo, an associate of the network and a senior manager at the bank, as a major player in money-laundering. Investigators have recovered substantial evidence of offshore accounts and fraudulent transactions linked to the group. The criminal syndicate's downfall has led to the incarceration of all key members, effectively dismantling their operations.

The article ended with a sad truth that Lorenzo had denounced in the past.

The present case has led to advocacy for increased transparency and accountability within financial institutions, and the implementation of more stringent regulations to mitigate future breaches.

The intricate web of lies Marina spun, coupled with the suffocating layers of corruption and backstabbing in his former workplace, solidified his decision to start anew. The stench of deceit was palpable.

He reflected on the unexpected twists that brought clarity to his path, turning towards Camila and Miguel with gratitude for the second chance they represented.

***

'No, no,' Miguel laughed, correcting Lorenzo's pronunciation. 'Like this—*guagua*. It means child in Quichua.'

His eyes sparkled with the joy of sharing his heritage, and Lorenzo felt his heart expand with a love that transcended blood ties.

Camila, watching from across the table, shook her head fondly.

'You're hopeless, *mi amor*,' she teased, reaching for his hand. 'But at least you're learning.'

Lorenzo grinned, ruffling Miguel's hair. 'One word at a time, querida. But I think I'm getting there.'

***

Their reunion transformed Lorenzo's established life in Ecuador into something richer, deeper.

After two years of building the micro-lending initiative, he had created a strong Foundation—now it became their shared mission, enhanced by Camila's diplomatic experience and deep understanding of her homeland.

'You've built something beautiful here,' Camila told him one evening, reviewing the Foundation's work. 'Now we can make it even stronger.'

Her connections and insight helped them expand their reach, particularly to communities that had been hesitant to trust formal banking structures.

Miguel adapted quickly to their new life, his natural resilience shining through. He took pride in watching his mother and Lorenzo work together, seeing how their different strengths created something greater than either could achieve alone. The Foundation's mission of helping others resonated with him, perhaps because he understood what it meant to need sanctuary.

They established their home in a location where the mountains themselves became their guardians. Lorenzo's years in Ecuador had taught him the value of discretion, and Camila's instincts for security proved flawless. Their work continued to grow, but they maintained their privacy through careful protocols and trusted intermediaries.

The Foundation evolved to include programs specifically designed to help families escape dangerous situations, drawing on their own experience.

Paolo managed the international connections from Rome, while they focused on building local relationships through their established networks. Their location remained known only to a handful of people, each vetted through years of proven loyalty.

Somewhere in Ecuador's vast landscape, between mountain and cloud forest, they created not just a hiding place, but a home.

The location became legend among those they helped—a place spoken of in whispers, known by its impact rather than its coordinates. Even those who benefited from their help never knew exactly where to find them; they were simply there when needed, like guardian angels operating in the shadows of the Andes.

**

Years went by.

Lorenzo found Camila and Miguel in the garden one evening, laughing together as they tended the flowers. The setting sun bathed the Andean peaks in gold as the evening wind delivered the intense fragrance of jasmine.

Their romance resembled a thrilling novel, fraught with peril, intensity, and insurmountable challenges. Ultimately, they had transformed their scars into strength, their fears into courage, and their past into a Foundation for helping others. Their shared life was a powerful testament to love's healing, transformative, and illuminating power, even during hardship.

Their story continued to unfold, each day adding new pages to their shared journey.

They married beneath Ecuador's endless sky, surrounded by friends who had become family. Miguel, now eighteen, officiating their wedding symbolised their journey from broken individuals to a united family, healing old wounds through trust and acceptance, his presence a symbol of their unconventional but unshakeable bond.

The Foundation they created flourished, offering hope and new beginnings to those trapped in organised crime's web, transforming their painful past into a source of light for others.

They documented cases like José, a repair shop owner who received his first legitimate loan, and Maria, who used their support to start a small textile business after years of struggle in the hands of loan sharks.

Their family grew with the arrival of Sofia and Mateo, whose laughter filled their home with joy that seemed impossible during those dark days in Rome. The children grew up hearing stories of courage and persistence, learning that love could bridge any distance and heal any wound.

The leather-bound journal Camila had given Lorenzo became a chronicle of their life together. Its pages held their story—the struggles, the triumphs, and the overwhelming love that had carried them through it all. Sometimes, they would read it together, marvelling at how far they had come from those uncertain days.

Occasional trips to Rome became pilgrimages of gratitude. Rosa, now reunited with her family for seven years, remained their guardian angel, becoming an aunt to their children and a cherished part of their expanding family circle.

***

One evening, as the sun painted the Ecuadorian sky in brilliant golds and purples, Lorenzo stood on their terrace, lost in contemplation. Camila found him there, wrapping her arms around him as they gazed at the horizon together.

'What are you thinking about, *mi amor*?' she asked softly.

'How grateful I am for this life we've built,' he replied, meeting her eyes. 'I wouldn't change a moment.'

Her smile held the warmth of a thousand sunsets.

'Neither would I. Our journey hasn't always been easy, but it's been worth every step to be here with you.'

They remained hand in hand, watching the sun dip behind the mountains that had once hidden their love.

Their narrative showcased human resilience, exceeding a simple romance.

***

One morning Lorenzo found his kids in the garden, Miguel teaching his younger siblings to make paper boats while Camila harvested herbs for dinner.

The afternoon light turned everything golden, and for a moment, the sight stole his breath—this family he never expected to have, this life built from the ashes of secrets and lies.

Sofia, barely five, launched her boat in the fountain with a squeal of delight. 'Papa, look! It floats!'

'Like the boats in the harbour at Guayaquil,' Miguel added, helping Mateo fold another craft. 'Remember when we went there last summer, *Papa*?'

The title still warmed Lorenzo's heart each time he heard it.

He remembered that trip—how Miguel had pointed out every detail to his younger siblings, proud to share his homeland with them. How Camila had squeezed his hand as they watched their children race along the waterfront, free from fear.

'Your technique has improved,' he told Sofia, examining her boat. 'Soon you'll be building entire fleets.'

'Like the Spanish galleons that brought gold,' Mateo piped up, his history lessons mixing with imagination.

'Or like the fishing boats that shelter in the cove below us during storms,' Camila added, her voice soft but pointed.

Their children might inherit their past, but they were determined to give them a future built on hope rather than fear.

***

The morning post brought a single envelope, pristine white with no return address. Inside, on heavy cream paper, a message in elegant Italian script:

Beloved friends, How beautiful your garden looks from the mountains. The children grow so strong, like the jacaranda trees. Sofia has her mother's grace, Mateo his father's smile. Such joy you've built here, so far from Rome. A pity that light casts the darkest shadows. Some debts remain unpaid. Some betrayals unforgiven. The storm season approaches.

Until we meet again.

The letter bore no signature, but the small phoenix watermark suggested there had not been a true ending, but a pause in an ongoing story. Lorenzo's hands trembled as he folded the paper, his eyes meeting Camila's worried ones across their sun-filled kitchen.

The children's laughter echoed from the garden, innocent and free.

For now.

AUTHOR'S NOTE

Writing *Chiaroscuro* began with a simple question: How do we see what society has rendered invisible?

Chiaroscuro, in Italian art, is the technique of using light and shadow to give paintings depth. The novel consistently juxtaposes wealth with poverty, power with vulnerability, and corruption with integrity. But most essentially, it distinguishes between those who are in the spotlight and those who are not.

The story of Lorenzo, Camila, and Miguel (but also Rosa) emerged from years of observing how financial systems can either uplift or oppress communities. Through my research into microfinance initiatives and conversations with immigrant families, especially in Rome, Buenos Aires and Riyadh, I discovered countless stories of resilience, ingenuity, and hope. Rosa's network of domestic workers who "see everything, hear everything" was inspired by real informal support systems that help marginalised communities survive and thrive.

While *Chiaroscuro* is a work of fiction, its themes reflect real challenges faced by immigrants and vulnerable populations worldwide.

The corruption Lorenzo uncovers exists in various forms, as do the quiet heroes who fight it. For every Bianchi who exploits desperation, countless individuals are working to create ethical alternatives.

This novel is dedicated to those who refuse to remain invisible, build bridges between worlds, and choose love over fear. May their stories continue to emerge from shadow into light.

THANK YOU FOR READING!

If you enjoyed *Chiaroscuro*, please consider leaving a review on your preferred platform. Your feedback helps independent authors reach new readers.

For updates on future releases and behind-the-scenes insights into the research that shaped this novel, you can follow me on:

- Goodreads: https://www.goodreads.com/rondanini

- Website: https://www.rondanini.com

Thank you for joining Lorenzo, Camila, and Miguel on their journey.

ACKNOWLEDGEMENT

A special thank you goes to

- *Frank Booth* for his help and input and to

- My friend and former boss, *Dave Axtell*, for supporting me and pushing me to complete this work.

I also want to thank my brother-in-law, *Silvio,* who, many years ago, instilled in me the idea of writing a book about the struggles of the immigrant communities in Rome.

But the enormous thank you goes to *all the people* who happened to cross paths with me, many by pure coincidence, and who made me a storyteller.

ABOUT THE AUTHOR

Luigi Pascal Rondanini

The author also writes as Pascal De Napoli.

Luigi Pascal Rondanini's determination and tenacity in pursuing his ideals pushed him to leave his native Naples to pursue the opportunities offered by the world.

Born in November 1967 and raised in the capital of Campania, from a young age he cultivated a passion for writing and politics. The desire for social justice led him to actively engage in social issues and write literary works inspired by these values.

At a very young age, he moved abroad to the United Kingdom, where he embarked on a brilliant career in the financial sector and continued his passion for writing, infusing his works with social and political themes with courage and frankness.

Despite living in London, Rondanini has never lost the connection with his Neapolitan roots after having lived on five continents. In his writings, Neapolitan culture and identity emerge vividly as an example of cultural diversity that enriches humanity.

Rondanini wants to inspire readers to pursue their dreams with courage and determination. His story demonstrates how, with commitment and sacrifice, you can achieve great goals while remaining true to yourself and your values.

Rondanini is also a narrator and an Audiobook publisher for other authors.

Printed in Great Britain
by Amazon